MW01128614

All Too Familiar

Accidental Familiar 1

By Belinda White

Copyright 2019 Belinda White
KDP Print Edition

Chapter 1

"Stop right there!" I put every bit of power I could muster into that command. Not that it really helped.

The hulking pile of muscles masquerading as a man in front of me turned and looked at me. His eyes were wide and his mouth slightly open. An obvious look of disbelief if ever there was one.

Yeah, I get that a lot. Especially in my new line of work.

I'm five feet six inches—if I'm wearing two-inch heels—and not all that physically impressive. Most people, like the hulk here, would think that meant I was a lightweight. They were wrong, but that's what they would think.

Genius here was no exception to that rule of thumb.

"You really think you are going to take me in?" he snarled. Then he laughed. "I'm special forces, lady." The emphasis he put on that last word was more than a little creepy.

My head tilted as my eyes traveled over him. "Actually, you are ex-special forces."

He grunted. "No such thing. Once you're in, you're in for life." Then his look changed as he glanced around at our somewhat remote location and the distinct lack of people gained his attention. A slow smile started up on his face.

A smile that quickly turned into a leer. Time to nip that in the bud. Things weren't going to progress the way he thought they were. He might very well end up on the ground with me on top of him, but I could guarantee him that we'd still both have all our clothes on.

While he was still gathering himself for his lunge, I held up one hand toward him. He stopped, the incredulous look back.

"You didn't give me a chance to answer your first question. You know the one about why I think I am going to take you in?"

He grinned at me. "So, answer already. We got all night, babe." That leer again. Maybe it would freeze there to show the people who still supported this jerk the kind of man he really was.

I held up one finger. "Well, for one, you're drunk. In case you didn't know, being drunk can play a bit with your reflexes and your powers of observation,"

He glanced around quickly. "My sight is just fine, sweetie." He motioned to the emptiness of the alley we were currently in. "We're all alone here. Not all that much to observe, is there?"

The beast just wasn't taking the hint. As far as he was concerned, I wasn't a threat to his continued freedom. I liked it that way. Made my job a whole lot easier.

"For two," I continued, holding up the second finger as if he hadn't interrupted. "I'm quite good at mixed martial arts. I've even been known to do a few cage fights back in the day. And I keep up with it too."

He actually laughed. "I'll go in a cage with ya, darling. In fact, my current place is a lot like a cage. We could go there. I like a girl with a bit of fight to her."

Then he was going to love me.

My third finger went up. "Three, my last name happens to be Ravenswind. Perhaps you've heard of us?"

Okay, that got his attention. For the first time, he actually looked like he had a bit of doubt. What can I say? My family is kind of famous.

What counted more than my last name, however, was the fact that his gaze went back to my upheld hand every time I held up another finger. Only for a second, but a second was all I needed.

As I held up that critical fourth finger and his eyes went to my left hand, my right hand pulled my taser. There really isn't much aiming involved with that type of weapon, and once I had it drawn, I pulled the trigger without hesitation. He never saw what hit him.

A second later, I stood over him looking down at his now twitching and drooling body. "And four, I happen to have a taser."

I flipped him over facedown—much easier said than done—and applied zip ties to his wrists and ankles. Special Forces or no, he wasn't going anywhere until the police arrived, and I did the handover.

My friend Opie hadn't been happy when I'd accepted this job. After all, I had kind of announced that I was giving up the whole bounty hunter gig. But Boswell Bonds had made me an offer I couldn't refuse.

The payment for this job wasn't in cash. It was the one thing I needed most in the whole wide world. A car. Of course, I hadn't seen it yet, but that didn't worry me.

The town's mechanic had checked it out for me and had said it was in perfect running order, and only five years old. Practically new. I was trying not to think of the laughter in his voice as he'd told me that, though. There was definitely something there I was missing. It was a Boswell deal after all. The man always came out ahead of the game.

When Opie showed up in his squad car, I stood back and watched as he and another deputy started trying to manhandle the bail jumper into the back of their vehicle. The beast fought them, even with all his limbs somewhat restrained. Couldn't have that. Opie might get hurt.

I held up one hand toward the perp and gave him a brilliant smile. "I'm running a bit late here, so I'd very much appreciate it if you would cooperate with the deputies here. If not…" I used that upright hand to point down to the taser I was still holding.

Drunk or not, the beast finally took the hint that his fugitive days were over. Once he was in the car, Opie signed the custody paperwork for me, and I was done.

Another fugitive successfully found and detained by Amethyst Ravenswind. Maybe I'd given this up as a career too soon. I was getting pretty dang good at it.

***

In this mixed-up world, there are witches and then there are witches. The first variety are regular, ordinary humans that worship nature and use its many bounties to concoct potions, herbal remedies, and yes, even spells.

The problem is that most ordinary humans have even less magic flowing through their bodies than I do. And trust me, that isn't much.

Their potions and remedies may work, but they aren't going to have that extra special oomph. That oomph requires magic. Real magic. The kind that is passed from generation to generation through one's bloodlines.

For what it's worth, the magic in my family is extremely strong. Which makes me a huge disappointment to my aunt.

The exact opposite is true of my cousin Ruby. She's a heck of a witch. I've always thought that as we were both born on the same day, and at the same time, that somehow my magic had mistakenly been given to her.

It's the only way I can make sense of my lack of power. In the entire history of the Ravenswind family, I was an anomaly. A single almost magic-less witch in generations upon generations. I could understand Aunt Opal's extreme disappointment in me. After all, why should such an atrocity have to happen in the generation that she happened to rule?

Luck of the draw, I guess. Or maybe it had something to do with the fact that she and my mother had timed my birth to coincide with my cousin Ruby's. And the fact that Ruby had struggled her way to beat me into the world by a whopping two minutes.

What can I say? Ruby's always been more competitive than me. Even as a newborn.

So that led me to be the woman I am today. A witch, but a whole lot more on the human side than the magical one. I could still do spells and potions, but they lacked that special something that the rest of my family's crafts had. I could live with that. Not that I really had a choice in the matter.

The fact remained that even one hundred percent human witches could get their brewing license if they were good enough. It was just a piece of paper sanctioned by the witches' council, but it held a lot of weight in our world. If you were going to get a decent price for your work, you needed that license.

There was a proctored test involved, which I'd been studying and preparing for. It had been a long and hard road, but I had the required testing spell and potion down to a science. Which, in more than one way, it really was.

I was as ready as I'd ever be. If all went well, after today, I'd be able to supplement my meager finances with yet another tiny stream of income. When you're as broke as I am most days, every tiny stream mattered. A lot.

Running into the beast on the way to the testing lab had been unexpected, to say the least. I'd almost passed up the opportunity to take him down. But the smarter part of me had put a stop to that kind of thinking. As much as passing this test might mean to me, I really needed that car.

I just hated that it ran me so far behind schedule. That wasn't even counting the fact that I wasn't nearly as calm, cool, and collected as I had been when I left my house.

Running late always gets my motor running in the wrong way.

Still, I managed to be on time, if just barely. The ingredients for my test were all laid out on the little kitchen counter. I took a couple of deep breaths to center myself and turned to the doorway. The witch proctors were a very punctual lot.

When my aunt Opal stepped into the room, I knew that I was doomed. No way was I getting my license to brew today.

There were four different examiners for this particular test. For the record, my aunt wasn't one of them. Just another example of how bad my luck truly is.

One by one, I shoved the ingredients I had assembled on the counter back into my oversized bag. I could feel the heat of Aunt Opal's glare on my back.

"Just like you to give up before you even try," she said.

I turned and met her eyes. "Even if I aced this brew, we both know you still wouldn't give me the license." I paused, but she never blinked an eye. Or denied my statement, either. "So why would I waste perfectly good herbs when you plan to fail me, anyway?"

She closed her eyes and shook her head. "Do you really think you are ready for your license?"

She would ask. We both knew I wasn't ready. It had taken me months of practice to master this spell and potion. And they weren't even difficult ones. Level one witchcraft at best.

But then with the tiny amount of magic I possessed, I'd never be any more ready than I was today. I was sensing it wasn't a coincidence that my aunt was filling in as a proctor today. She'd known I was up for testing.

"You know your magic would be stronger with a familiar." Just like good ole Opal to start that up again.

I nodded slowly. "So would my allergies."

Opal chewed her lower lip. "A familiar doesn't have to be a cat, you know."

I just looked at her. Yes, my allergies flared up worse around cats, but dogs weren't exactly a walk in the park, either. At least with them, the allergy medicine I took on a daily basis was enough to keep me from sneezing myself into a frenzy. With cats, the medicine didn't even make a dent.

"Or a dog," she said frowning. She might not be able to read my mind, but I've never discounted the possibility that she could. "I've heard that rats are quite intelligent."

Shivers ran over me from head to toe. No way was I creating a personal bond with a rat. No freaking way.

I hefted the now heavy bag onto my shoulder and walked out of the testing kitchen. There just wasn't anything left to say.

Chapter 2

The day before hadn't quite lived up to my expectations, that was true. But that minor setback—okay major setback in my magical dealings—still wasn't enough to keep me from jumping out of bed this morning with a spring in my step.

Today was the day I became a car owner. A day I'd been looking forward to for years. All I had to do was turn in the paperwork to Boswell, pick up the keys, and take a short trip to the Bureau of Motor Vehicles to get it all legal and road ready.

I was pumped.

Even the fact that there was a full-blown coven meeting tonight wasn't enough to put a damper on me. Not today. In retrospect, I probably should have joined Ruby on her singles' retreat. The prospect of spending the night dancing around a bonfire on the top of a hill surrounded by trees wasn't all that appealing. Even less so considering it would be just me and Opal.

Times like this I really just wish my mom would come home already. It'd already been a full year. Surely, she hadn't left me alone with Opal forever. Had she? It was beginning to look like it.

I was just buttoning up my flannel shirt when there was a knock on my bedroom door.

Opening the door revealed Opal standing out in the hallway. "I wanted to talk to you about tonight."

I smiled at her. This could only be good news, right? Like she'd come to see the silliness of holding a bonfire coven meeting with only two witches in attendance?

"I was thinking maybe we should just cancel the meeting tonight. I'm guessing you think so too?"

She looked affronted. I could quickly tell that calling off the bonfire was not something she had even considered doing. So why was she standing in my doorway? I waited.

"It's the full moon. Witches show their gratitude to the God and Goddess on the full moon." Her voice held more than a touch of rebuking. "You know that. How many of us show up is irrelevant."

I took a deep breath. Well, it had been a short-lived hope after all. "Then what did you want to talk about?"

Her eyes left mine to focus on the wall behind me. Not a good sign. "I've invited the Windsong Coven to join us tonight."

My eyebrows shot up. She'd done what? The Windsong Coven had asked to join our monthly bonfires before. Numerous times. And every time, Opal had declined. She must have really felt that her back was to the wall to actually call and invite them.

But then, without them, we would have been just two witches dancing naked around a fire. Now, at least, there would be more of us.

She must have taken my silence as a sign of disapproval.

"Is that a problem?"

I shook my head. "No, not at all." Then I thought quickly. I was okay with being naked with just me and Opal, but the Windsong Coven had a few male witches, and I wasn't at all sure how comfortable that made me feel. "Although I should warn you, I plan to wear a swimsuit tonight."

If I'd been expecting an argument, I didn't get one. "I can understand that. That suit of yours shows plenty enough skin to count as skyclad as far as I'm concerned."

Well, yeah, bikinis usually do. That was my whole point. I could cover the bits I wanted covered and still honor the Divine Ones.

Her eyes finally made it back to mine. "You getting ready to go somewhere? This early?"

I nodded. "I pick up my car today, remember?"

She closed her eyes and shook her head. Then she left.

Don't worry, Aunt Opal, I thought. I won't take your parking spot. But you won't be the only one with wheels in the family anymore.

Joint coven meeting or not, I was still pumped.

There was a reason I was up and ready so early. Boswell had left the car at the mechanics for me to pick up. That meant two stops for me. The first to Boswell Bonds to finalize everything and get the keys, and then on to take possession of the vehicle. I knew it was a 2014 Dodge Challenger, and I'd looked them up online and fallen very deeply in love with the whole look of it. I couldn't believe my good fortune.

The book value of the car was a whole heck of a lot more than Boswell ever would have parted with money wise. From what I understood, it had been the Beast's primary vehicle before he'd handed it over to the bondsman for bail money. And now it would be mine.

I'd be worried that Boswell was pulling something, but I trusted Eddie the mechanic. He wouldn't steer me wrong. For one thing, he was a believer in the power of my family.

Not all townspeople were. Some thought we were just crazy eccentrics that liked to dance naked in the moonlight.

Now and then, like on the days of the full moon, I had to agree they might have something there. After all, we could be both powerful witches—well most of us—and crazy eccentrics, too, right? The two didn't have to be mutually exclusive.

I paused at the little locked lean-to under the outside stairs, took a deep breath, and kept walking. Yes, I would much rather take my bike and cut the time the trip would take me by more than half, but I just didn't think the bike would fit into the trunk of my new car. No way was I leaving my bike behind. I might not want to depend on it for primary transportation, but I still loved every inch of it.

Squaring my shoulders, I started walking. By now the sun was well and truly up and the day was actually turning out to be pleasantly warm. For once, the breeze was quiet, letting the sun's warmth do its job.

I hadn't made it half a mile before Opie's personal car, an old Chevy Nova that he thought was the pure embodiment of all things manly, pulled up beside me.

"Want a lift?" He was grinning from ear to ear.

I glanced down the open road and then back to him. Something was up, but if it saved me having to walk a few miles, I was game.

"Sure, thanks." I got in and buckled up then turned to him. "What brings you out this way, anyway?"

If anything, his grin just got bigger. "You're going to get your car, right? I just wanted to be there when you did." He chuckled. "Don't be surprised if half the town turns out for this."

Okay, I knew I was excited about the day, but half the town? What the heck?

I glared at him. "Spill."

His chuckle grew into a full-fledged belly laugh. "And spoil the surprise? Not on your life."

Worry crept into my brain. "Is there something wrong with the car? Eddie said it ran great."

"Oh, it does. It does. Runs great. Only has about fifty thousand miles on it, too, so it should last you for a very long time." That idea seemed to set him off again. I was beginning to wish I'd just opted to walk.

"I have to go to Boswell's first to turn in the paperwork and get the keys," I reminded him.

"No problem. It's my day off. I have all day to enjoy this. Can't think of anywhere else in the entire world I'd rather be right now."

Now the worry had a firm hold.

Within minutes—which shows how much time a car can save a person—we were parked on the street outside Boswell Bonds. Opie stayed in the car while I went in to do the paperwork.

I'd figured Boswell would be all frowns. He always was whenever he was handing me my pay for doing a job. Not this morning. The whole dumb grinning thing must be all the new rage in town.

"You need a lift over to the garage?"

The weasel was offering me a lift? When had he ever offered to do something nice for someone without making a profit off it? That one little question had my worry going off the charts. What the heck was wrong with this car?

I declined, grabbed the keys, and went back out to Opie. Somehow, it didn't really surprise me when Boswell followed me out the door and walked furiously down the street towards the garage. I'd never seen the man move that fast. He'd most likely be there before we would.

When we pulled into the little parking area for the shop, I could tell that Opie hadn't been far from wrong. It certainly looked like at least half the town had shown up for this. There was a feeling of happiness and suspense in the air, like carnival day or something.

They actually cheered when I got out of the car. Huh. That had never happened to me before.

Eddie made his way through the crowd and motioned for me to follow him around behind his building. As excited as I was, the dread was still creeping in. First Opie, then Boswell, now the rest of the town?

But my feet didn't fail me, and I followed Eddie toward my new set of wheels.

When I first saw it, my heart was in my throat. The love was instant and overwhelming. The Beast had sprung for a custom paint job. I'd never expected that. The car was a mixture of green, black, and white, all swirled together in a camouflage pattern. I loved it!

My sharp intake of breath set Opie off again. "Wait for it," he said. I wasn't sure if he was talking to me or the crowd.

Eddie had been standing in front of me blocking part of my view of the vehicle. When he stepped to the side, I swear the entire town held its breath. Finally, I saw why everyone had shown up for this.

The Beast had owned a construction company, and within several of the black spaces on the car, there were slogans. And symbols. The driver's side door held the biggest of them, at least from this side. "Connor Construction keeps going until the job is done." That wasn't so very bad, but the little picture to the side was. An overly tall standing screwdriver flanked at the bottom by huge nuts—the hardware kind, at least. It left no doubt as to exactly what 'job' Connor had been referring to.

I swallowed hard and made a complete circuit around the car. There were more slogans and pictures than I have fingers and toes. I had two choices. I could be upset that I would be driving a vehicle that basically degraded women everywhere with overblown masculinity and downright obscenity, or I could be overjoyed that I had a vehicle to drive. I went with the latter.

After all, from a distance, all you really noticed was the camouflage pattern. And that I loved.

When I didn't burst into tears and run away sobbing, the disappointed crowd started to leave. Must not have been nearly as much fun for them as they'd hoped. Boswell, however, stuck around.

"So, how do you like it?" Funny, but the grin he was still wearing was so out of place it was totally starting to freak me out.

"Well, I'm guessing you can see that it needs a bit of work."

"Nope. It really doesn't need a thing. Perfect just the way it is. Isn't that right, deputy?"

Opie looked deep into my eyes. "You know Boswell. I think in her eyes, it pretty much is."

See? At least one person here got me. I reached out and touched the car for the first time. "It's really mine?"

Now even Boswell had lost interest. Maybe the fact that he'd just given away an actual car that was worth much more than any cash payment he would have given me was finally starting to seep into that thick skull of his.

Too late. This sweet ride was mine. I'd deal with the slogans later.

Shouldn't be too hard.

Chapter 3

The rest of the morning passed by very slowly. The BMV must exist in some kind of time loop. I'd swear I was there for longer than the three hours it took me. Not that three hours was anything to sneeze at. But I walked out legal to drive my new baby and that's all that mattered.

I wanted nothing more than to take her for a real spin. Spend the whole rest of the day venturing as far away from Wind's Crossing as I could make it in the hours I had left. But that was just a wish. The meeting tonight would be a long one, and I'd need a nice nap this afternoon if I even hoped to be able to cope with not only my aunt, but the entire Windsong Coven as well.

If only I could go back in time and go on that retreat with Ruby. Why should she have all the fun? And more importantly, why should I be stuck at home alone with her mom? Sometimes life just wasn't fair.

So I settled for a quick drive through lunch and then made one final stop of the day. I felt a lot better after ordering two magnet signs advertising my photography services. They would work nicely to cover up the rather graphic symbol and slogan on my car doors. I even ordered a nice witch flying across a full moon decal for my hood. That was another few feet of car space I wouldn't have to worry about.

Besides, everyone in town knew we were witches, anyway. It wasn't like I had anything to hide in that respect.

I was halfway home when I remembered the donuts. Good thing I had my car. Having to double back to town when you're on a bicycle isn't fun. I could get used to this new freedom. Although I'd have to come up with some other way to get my daily exercise in. Pedaling to and from town was about the only physical workout I ever got.

Luckily, at this time of day, the Flour Pot wasn't busy. In the mornings, it could be murder just getting a donut and a cup of java. But after the lunch hour, it wasn't so bad. Of course, the donut selection was pretty skimpy by then too. That might be a part of it. I was really hoping he had a few raspberry-filled ones left. If not, I'd never hear the end of it.

Naomi Hill was at the counter when I walked in. If I hadn't desperately needed those donuts, I would have walked right back out again. It wasn't bad enough that she was fervent in her hatred of witches and everything they represented.

No, I'd added to that hatred by chasing down her precious son and putting him back in jail. Now, she hated witches in general and me in particular. I kept my head down, but she still saw me. I was really hoping she wasn't going to make a scene.

The thing was, there was only one raspberry donut left in the case, and I didn't want to take the chance of losing it. I stepped up to the counter and smiled at the man behind it. "I don't suppose you have any more Raspberry Delights in the back? You know they're my aunt's favorite."

"Sorry, Amie. Mrs. Hill took all the rest I had except that one. Opal will just have to make do with one."

She wasn't going to be happy, but at least I wasn't going home completely empty-handed. I could feel Mrs.

Hill's heated stare boring into my back. Dang it, she was still here. Probably wishing like heck that she'd taken that last Raspberry Delight.

At least she waited until after I placed my order to accost me. As I grabbed my bag and tried to hustle out the door, she stepped into my path.

"Well, look what the devil let out to play." Her tone was sharp. I knew if we hadn't been indoors, she'd have spit at my feet. It wouldn't be the first time.

"You know we aren't devil worshipers, Mrs. Hill. In fact, we worship the same God I believe you do." It wasn't my fault she failed to worship the Goddess too.

Her bark of a laugh had not an ounce of humor to it. "I highly doubt that. Your whole family is nothing but pagans." She said that like it was a bad thing.

Goddess help me, I just couldn't hold myself in. "So, how's Tommy doing?" Last I'd heard he was still serving time in the local jail for hacking into places he shouldn't have been able to access. He always was a geek when it came to computers.

"Like you don't know, you hussy." The hatred in her eyes burned straight into my soul. "Back off him, witch. Opal cast her spell on my George back in high school and left me with nothing but the dregs of a diabetic man when she was through with him. If you know what's good for you, you'll release your spell on my Tommy. A woman can only take so much."

I was still standing there with my mouth open when the door shut behind her. What the heck? I turned to Mr. Clark, the shop owner, and luckily only other witness to her even odder than usual behavior.

"What bee flew in her bonnet today? You have any idea at all what she's talking about?"

He shrugged. "Full moon's tonight, ain't it? Probably wondering how she'll keep the mister home tonight."

"I take it he's found our new meeting place then."

"Oh yeah. Don't matter how many times you all move around, he'll keep looking 'til he finds you." He blushed and turned his eyes away. "You gotta admit a family of attractive female witches dancing in the buff around a fire is quite the draw."

"Well, for the record, most nights I dance in a swimsuit."

He nodded. "Heard that." Then he grinned. "Kind of disappointed me to be truthful. But then it ain't you young girls George Hill is going to see."

I thought back to Naomi's words. "Was there really something between Opal and George?"

"Not nearly as much as George would have liked there to be."

A couple of people walked in the shop and Mr. Clark turned to help them. I raised my bag in thanks and left.

Learn something new every single day.

***

When my alarm went off at seven, the last thing I wanted to do was get up. Not that I was still super tired or anything. I just didn't want to do the next few hours of my life. If only time travel existed, I could zap myself into the next morning and not have to deal with a joint coven meeting.

I was really starting to think that the great and powerful Opal Ravenswind had made a huge mistake inviting the Windsong gang. They might think this was a victory and the start to many more joint meetings. I'm not sure that was in the cards. Like ever.

My swimsuit went on first, then I layered on a clean pair of pajamas—hey, I didn't care what the others thought of me, and they were so much easier to get out of. It wasn't like we were going any distance. Just into the woods out back and up the big hill. We used to meet in the valley, but we got tired of having so many men camp out in the woods surrounding us. Most of them even brought high-powered binoculars. The hills around that valley weren't on Ravenswind land, and we couldn't control who camped out there to watch the festivities.

We had moved up to the top of the hill hoping to stop that. Didn't sound like it worked though. Perverts will always find a way. I just didn't like the idea of being anyone's peep show. Even if he wasn't doing it to look at me, I was still there. A swimsuit was most likely going to be my go-to skyclad outfit from here out. I might even have to invest in a one piece just for the occasion.

After dressing, I grabbed a couple bundles of firewood and went to join Opal. She was already there, preparing herself for what lay ahead. That was her job. My job was building the fire and making sure it was going strong by ten o'clock when the others showed up. I'm thinking Opal's job was a lot easier.

I already had a pretty good pile of dead wood up there that I'd gathered over the last couple of days. The two bundles I grabbed should be more than enough to see us through the meeting. Too big of a fire and I'd be up there for hours after the meeting waiting for the embers to finally die down. The last thing we wanted was to commune with the Goddess' nature and then burn it down. That would really put a damper on her blessings.

I brought my latest mystery novel to read while the fire was doing its thing. If I sat just right, with my back to Opal, she'd never know I wasn't meditating like she was. Of course, once it started getting dark, that would be over.

Not that it mattered. Val showed up just before nine. The fire was already going pretty nicely, so to my mind, that was okay. Opal, however, wasn't happy. Especially when the other members of her coven traipsed in behind her. And each and every one of them was in full witch garb, including what they must have taken as a prerequisite: a full length hooded cloak.

I had to turn to hide my grin. What must they be thinking of me and Opal just standing here in regular old clothes? Well, actually I was still in my pajamas, but Opal had opted for an oversized mu-mu type of house dress. One that would be easy to discard when it was time for the dancing to start. Knowing Val, she and her clan didn't have a stitch on under those cloaks.

Val gave Opal a smile that didn't nearly reach her eyes. "Hope you don't mind we're early, but we wanted the full experience. I figured you'd be here hours earlier."

Well, yeah, did she think fires just popped into existence all by themselves? But I didn't think the fire was why she was early. She was afraid Opal was going to call down the blessings before they got there.

"Fine. Park your asses on the ground and meditate for an hour. That's my full experience in a nutshell." Then my aunt closed her eyes, shutting out the intruders to her concentration and returning to her trance state. She was great at that. Shutting out others, I mean.

I shoved my book into my backpack and went back to tending the fire. Knowing my aunt, her calm facade wasn't going to last too much longer. We'd be starting early for sure.

The real shocker to me was when Tommy Hill showed up a few minutes later.

Val must not be all that into meditation, which for a witch says a lot, because she knew the instant he stepped into the clearing. She glanced over at Opal who, for all the world to see, was still in a trance state. At least that's what it looked like. I could see the pulse jumping in her neck. She wasn't nearly as relaxed as she appeared to be.

And now, neither was I.

Tommy made it past the other sitting members of the coven to me. "I'm really sorry about this. When I asked for an invitation, I honestly didn't know it would be a joint meeting with your coven."

I was trying hard to not meet his eyes. They say that our eyes are the windows to our souls. And right now, my soul was very conflicted. So I went back to safer ground for me.

"I thought you were still in jail." We were keeping our voices low. So low that it was my hope the crackling of the fire would mask our conversation to the others.

He smiled at me. "Let's just say I made a deal while I was inside."

"Let me guess. The government needed your help on some super-secret hacking project that only you could do?" Sue me, I watch a lot of crime shows on television. That was how it usually went on them.

His smile faded. "I'm not supposed to talk about that."

My eyes flew to his. "You mean that's what really happened?"

He wouldn't meet my eyes, instead he looked over at the meditating witches. "I never said that, did I?"

Okay. Maybe real life mimics fiction more than I thought. After all, I was a bounty hunter now. Who could have seen that coming? I tried going back to a safer subject, even if it was a more uncomfortable one for me.

"So, you're a member of the Windsong Coven now? Where's your cloak? And, most importantly, what's your mom think about that?" After my run-in with her earlier in the day, I was fairly sure I knew the answer to that last question.

He blushed. "I'm not a member. Not yet, anyway. I just wanted to see what it was all about, you know." He threw a glance my way. "I guess I kind of wanted to know what made you who you are." He paused. "And Valerie loaned me a cloak, but I forgot it in my closet back home. Didn't want to go by and get it with Mom there."

I just stared at him. "Wait a minute." I had to force my voice even lower. "You aren't a member? You mean Val Kimble invited a guest to a joint meeting with the Gemstone Coven?"

That was so not cool. And there was absolutely no way Aunt Opal would allow it if she knew. You invite curious guests to a regular meeting. Full moon blessings were meant only for those who were already dedicated and experienced witches.

Now I was torn. Did I tell Opal and have her create a huge scene, or keep quiet and plead ignorance when she eventually found out? I mean, we were talking about Opal here. She would find out.

Maybe there was another way. I motioned for Tommy to follow me, and I walked off into the trees. No way did I want the others, especially Opal, to overhear this.

Once we were far enough out of earshot, I turned to the hot geek standing beside me. "Look, Tommy, I hope you don't take this the wrong way, but you really need to leave before things get out of hand."

His eyebrows knit together as he frowned at me. "Do these meetings really get that wild?"

I laughed. "Oh, heck no." Then I remembered my mission and sobered. "But the Gemstone Coven has very strict rules that obviously aren't the same as the Windsong Coven. We don't allow non-witches to attend full blown Bringing Down the Moon meetings. Those are strictly for witches only." I tried to look sad about it, but part of my distress was the fact that if Tommy stayed, chances were good I'd be getting a closeup view of his dangling private parts. As nice as that might be, I really wasn't ready for that.

"I see." He was quiet for a minute, looking deep into my eyes. "If I leave tonight, do you think Opal would invite me to one of your regular meetings?"

Good question. "You think I know what my aunt would do? That's never been the case. But I can promise I'll put in a good word for you, for whatever that's worth." I glanced back in the direction of the group. "But you really need to leave now."

"He's staying." I jumped as the voice came from directly behind me. I whirled to find Valerie standing there.

Dang, those cloaks served some sort of purpose after all. They made the wearers practically invisible in the twilight.

"And I say he's going." Opal had joined the party. My heart started racing even more than it had been from Val's sudden appearance. This was so what I'd been hoping to avoid.

"Tommy Hill is a guest of the Windsong Coven, and I say he stays." Val paused. "You do realize that he will make the thirteenth person here, right?"

"Thirteen is a powerful number, yes, but only if all thirteen are witches. He is not." Opal jerked her head toward Tommy, and he flinched. "Having that number of dancers would by no means appease the Goddess for having a non-believer at a sacred meeting."

Val made a face and took a step toward Opal. "And who are you to speak for what the Goddess wants?"

I swallowed and took a step back, dragging Tommy with me. That was the absolute wrong question to ask. Val was on her own now.

Opal swelled in stature. I could recognize a spell at work, but I heard Tommy's sudden intake of breath. Yeah, we pretty much try to keep our magical abilities out of the public eye. But right now, Opal was far too pissed to care about little things like that.

"I am the Goddess' High Priestess of the Gemstone Coven. As such, I am her disciple and her spokeswoman." Opal's voice had a ringing quality that made it sound not quite human. The words echoed among the trees. Definitely a spell.

Val must be a brave woman, because she stood her ground. Even if she did look a bit unsure about it. "And I am the Goddess' High Priestess of the Windsong Coven." She glanced over at me. "And my coven has substantially more members than yours."

Opal gave a hollow laugh. "Numbers don't equate to power. If they did, you wouldn't have been so eager to join with us tonight. Which I now realize was a vast mistake. I think you all should leave." She stressed the word all.

But High Priestess number two just dug her heels in. Big mistake. Big, big mistake.

Tommy took a deep breath and stepped in between the two high ranking witches. "Look, I had no idea my presence here tonight would cause such hostility. I'm leaving." He looked at Opal. "I truly hope you don't allow this to disrupt your celebration of the Goddess."

And he left.

I was beginning to think Tommy Hill, or the Hot Geek as I also thought of him, was a very good man. Smart one, too, and with more than just computers.

It would be nice if I could say that Tommy's actions brought peace to the hillside, but that isn't what happened. When Opal gets riled, it isn't a matter of flipping a simple switch to return everything to normal again. It's a lengthy and time-consuming process.

Val's aggression and demands didn't help.

"Look," I said, trying out the role of peacemaker. "Why don't we go back and show the Goddess our appreciation now. Nothing that has happened here tonight has changed how we feel about Her, right?" Then I held my breath.

It took a solid minute but finally Opal nodded, and I could breathe again.

The rest of the meeting wasn't nearly as heartwarming and spontaneous as usual, but the power still flowed down upon us as we danced. It's weird, actually. I mean, I have like almost no magic in my entire body, and yet I can feel the power. As I said, that's weird, right? I've asked so many times why the Goddess would give me power and no way to use it.

She hasn't answered me yet, though.

I could tell from the questioning and ecstatic faces of the visiting witches that this wasn't the norm for them. Not that I was surprised by that. Opal had true magic. Val, I was beginning to think, had none.

Afterward, we sat hand in hand around the dwindling fire. I made sure I was between Opal and Val. Our numbers had dwindled by yet another by that time. Misty Rhodes, Val's second in command, had to leave early to relieve her babysitter. Too bad for her. This was my favorite time of the night. Sitting there, letting my heart rate return to normal and just breathing in the glorious remaining power.

It was a little piece of heaven.

Everything was right with the world. Right up until Valerie Kimble opened her mouth and ruined it. Obviously, she didn't get the whole sitting in the glory of the Goddess's blessings thing.

"That was amazing!" Her face was flushed with ecstasy, and she stretched and twisted, reveling in her newfound power. "When can we do this again?"

Opal laughed. "How's the twelfth of never work for you?"

"What?"

Opal's eyes were still closed. She wasn't going to grace Val with the entirety of her presence. "This was a onetime deal. Next month Ruby will be here, and we'll be back to our trinity." One eye opened and glanced over at Val. "Three's a pretty powerful number too, you know."

Val dropped my hand and for a minute I thought she was going to go for Opal's throat. Like I'd let that happen.

"It isn't right for your coven to keep all this power to yourselves. The Goddess would want it shared."

That got another laugh. "If the Goddess wants to share her blessings with you, she will. It doesn't matter if you're here or on your own bloody hillside."

She had a point. But not one Val was willing to accept. It was far easier to gather in the blessings of a powerful witch than to call down those blessings yourself. I felt her glance at me.

"Can't you talk some sense into her? We're all witches, and we can only grow stronger by banding together."

True for them, not for us. I kept my mouth shut. No way was I getting in the middle of this.

"Come, Windsong Coven. We're leaving."

They all stood up as one, which was actually kind of creepy. Then they followed her out toward the small path leading back down to the farmhouse and their cars. Val stopped just short of the path and doubled back to the small table I had set up to the side to hold the plate of donuts and a couple large thermos flasks of hot coffee and cocoa. I watched as she surveyed the table's offerings and then reached down, grabbed a donut, and left.

My heart sank. I had a funny feeling I knew exactly which donut she had chosen. And why.

Chapter 4

It was after three o'clock before I'd finally gotten to bed. Sleep didn't come for a while, either. The night had gone pretty much as I'd expected it to. My mind was still racing even if my body was trying to rest.

So, when my phone chirped at six, I wasn't exactly a happy camper. I mean who calls a witch this early on the morning after a full moon? Surely the normals have a clue about those kinds of things. Even Opal and Ruby's shop opens late on these mornings.

I wouldn't have answered it at all, but the distinctive ring tone told me it was most likely a job. I really couldn't afford to turn down the opportunity for some side money. Especially as the gigs coming from newspaper editor Rolly were a whole lot easier than the ones from Boswell Bonds. Safer too.

"This better be a job." My voice sounded a bit like sandpaper but only a couple hours of sleep and not enough hydration will do that to you.

"It is. Get dressed, grab your camera, and get your cute little red-headed behind over to Val Kimble's house."

Val's house? I started wondering if this phone call was a dream or something. Why would he be sending me there? My brain just couldn't come up with an answer to that.

"Are you moving yet? I need you there to get some pictures before they remove the body."

Swallowing the sudden lump out of one's throat is even harder when said throat is bone dry. "Body?"

"That's right. Her neighbor found her when she went to let out her dog. Still sitting in her car out in front of her house. So get a move on." The call ended, and I stared at the phone in horror.

Crap on toast. Val Kimble was dead? Heaven help me but the first thing I did was check to make sure Opal's car was still parked on the street. It was, thank the Goddess. Even more importantly, I could tell it hadn't been moved since yesterday afternoon. Of course, with Opal's power, that really didn't mean as much as it should. If anyone could kill someone miles away from the comfort of their own home, it was Opal Ravenswind.

I threw on a pair of black jeans and pulled a flannel shirt over the T-shirt I normally slept in. No time for the niceties like a bra. After a quick round in the bathroom to take care of a sudden pressing need, I grabbed my camera and hightailed my cute little red-headed behind over to Val's.

The Challenger really came in handy. I'm not sure at all that I could have made it on my bike. Not today. My balance wasn't all that good when I didn't get enough sleep. It was nice having the car doing the whole balancing thing for me. Of course, it had it much easier as it had four wheels, versus my bike's two.

My brain was reeling the entire way. Last night had been pretty ugly between Opal and Val. Now Val was dead?

That just so couldn't be good.

Please don't let Opal be involved. That was my new mantra as I drove the short distance into town and back out the other side towards Val's house. She lived out in the country too. About five miles the other side of town from us. She had married well, and her husband was one of our town's few attorneys. It was enough of a boost to give them a very nice home.

Unlike my family, who had opted for a little acreage to go with their home, her manor house was in a very upscale housing addition. Far too good to be found inside city limits, but no real green space to speak of, either. Rather odd for someone who called themselves a witch.

As I got closer, I wondered why her husband hadn't been the one to find her. Didn't he miss her when she didn't go to bed last night? Or maybe she had and just got up super early to run errands?

Even as tired as I was, I couldn't convince myself that was the case, no matter how much I wanted it to be. So my mantra changed. "Please let there be lots and lots of blood."

It might sound like an odd mantra, but if there was a lot of blood loss, that would rule out Opal in my eyes. I had absolutely no doubt in my mind that Opal could kill someone from a distance with magic. She was an extremely powerful witch. Even if our coven had a thousand members, I had no doubt that Opal would still be the most skilled, and thus the High Priestess. She was that good.

But magic would kill from the inside out. I couldn't see where that would lead to a lot of blood. Unless of course, a witch got inventive and tried to make it look like an accident.

Dang, maybe I couldn't rule out Opal after all, even if there was a river of the red stuff. I had a terrible feeling about all of this. The timing was just too convenient.

I turned into the housing addition and was immediately signaled to pull over by a sheriff's deputy. He came up to my driver's side window. "I'm sorry, ma'am, but you need to leave. This is a crime scene, and we need to keep the general public back."

Popping open my glove box, I pulled out the press pass badge the local paper had given me. "Does this help?"

"Sorry, ma'am, but it doesn't. No one gets in until we've processed the scene."

Luckily, that was when Opie showed up. I figured he'd give me the old heave-ho too, but he didn't. After he parked, he joined the officer at my window.

"You got your camera with you?"

I patted the bag on the seat next to me. "Right here. Rolly called and asked me to get some pictures for the front page."

He nodded. "Figured as much." Then he turned to the other deputy. "I'll take it from here. We're going to let her in under one condition." He eyes found mine and held on. "You run your pictures by us before you give them to Rolly. If we don't approve of one, you delete it—or give it to us for our use only."

My head tilted. "You need a crime scene photographer, don't you?"

He gave me a half-smile. "You always could see right through me."

After parking where he told me to, I walked over to the front of Val's house. About a half dozen law enforcement vehicles were lined up on the street, their lights flashing. The officers themselves were spread out, gathering evidence and taking photos with their phones. Yeah, they wouldn't get near the detail I could with my setup.

Sheriff Taylor, Opie's dad, saw me and nodded his approval. "Opie said you offered to help us out. I appreciate it. Your equipment is a lot better than anything we have here." He gestured to the car. "Can you handle this?"

I took a deep breath and nodded. "Is there a lot of blood?"

He shook his head. "Not a drop that we can see. We still aren't sure quite what's happened here. But for now, we aren't ruling anything out. Could have been a freak heart attack, but I want some good pictures before we move the body out for the coroner to take. I really appreciate your help here."

From the sound of it, Opie had left out the whole part about me being there to get pictures for the paper. That was more than fine by me. Two birds, one stone, the way I saw it.

Glancing around, there was one person I'd expected to see there that wasn't. "Um, sheriff? Where's Mr. Kimble? Is he going to be okay with me doing this?" I didn't want to have to deal with a grieving husband too.

"Haven't you heard? Mr. Kimble is in Bermuda with his secretary. I thought that little piece of gossip had made the full rounds by now. Guess not." A deputy came up with a question, and the sheriff gave me a final nod before walking away with him.

Things kind of made more sense to me now. Witches tend to lean on magic when things aren't going right in their life. Sounds like that was the case for Val. No wonder she wanted all the blessings she could get. Probably had a nice little revenge spell in mind.

Starting from where I was on the street, I began snapping photos. Of the ground, the sidewalk, the driveway, and the outside of her car. Her driver's side door was open, but I went all the way around the car before I got there. The photos would have meant more if I'd been able to take them before dozens of people's footprints littered the yard and area, but we'd have to make do with what we could get.

Once I got to the driver's side door, I took another deep breath. Then I changed out the lens for something a little more suited to close up work and captured the inside of the vehicle and the body in as much fine detail as I could.

I've been rumored to have a little magic when it comes to my photography. I don't really believe that, though. I've worked hard to gain my skills. It's just easier for people to think I use magic than to admit I'm really good at something. A lot of that probably has to do with my inability to keep a day job.

I started with the car itself. Front seat and back. If there was a killer that had been present, and they'd left anything behind, I definitely wanted it on virtual film. Especially as that would prove it wasn't Opal. My aunt wasn't the type to walk that far, no matter how upset she was.

Once I got everything but the body, I steeled myself and started in. The thing that was freaking me out the most was the fact that her eyes were still open, as if they were staring at me, begging me to save her. Only that wasn't a possibility now. The strongest magic in the world couldn't give life back to the dead. And that was probably a very good thing.

As I snapped, I found my eyes searching for Opal's mark. Magic always left a mark. The problem was, the mark didn't always show up in a visible place. As she was still wearing her all-encompassing cloak, only a very small part of her was visible. I was sure the sheriff didn't want me actually touching the body so that left a lot of skin open to being marked.

I was really regretting telling Opie about the whole spell mark thing. But as he was a dear and close friend, I had thought it important for him to know in his line of work. Hopefully, he had forgotten all about it. Or, at the very least, he wouldn't recognize the mark as Opal's.

Was that the right thought to have, though? Was I seriously thinking Opal had done this? And if so, did I really want her to get away with it? Murder was murder, even if a close family member did it.

Either way, I wasn't finding out this morning. The only odd thing about the body was a small amount of red at the corner of her mouth. It didn't really look like blood. I zoomed in on it and then took another glance at the passenger seat.

There was the raspberry donut she had taken from the treat table last night. It had a few bites taken from it, and the raspberry filling was showing. That was probably the red on her lip. Raspberry.

Crap. Had Opal cursed the donut? She hadn't said a word when she'd found out Val had taken it, but I had seen her face. That one little thing had probably been the final straw as far as Opal was concerned.

Had she killed Val Kimble over a single raspberry filled donut from the Flour Shop? Talk about your food to die for.

When Sheriff Taylor saw I was done, he came over to stand beside me.

"Heard there was a bit of a ruckus at that coven meeting of yours last night."

I nodded. Here we go. "There was. Mostly Val's fault, too, if I can say that."

He glanced inside the vehicle, then he motioned for his men to let the coroner in to start the process of removing the body. One look at all the men still milling around, and he pulled me to one side, out of earshot.

"I can't believe I'm going to ask this, but could a spell have done this? Killed her, I mean."

He had lowered his voice, so I did the same. "You know I'm not blessed in that department, sheriff. Opal would be able to answer that question better than I could."

"And yet, I'm asking you."

I glanced back at the car where the coroner was now blocking the view of the body. Doing his initial assessment of the situation just like all the crime shows I watched on television. Funny, but they had never captured the full emotion of that moment for me. Nothing like knowing the victim to bring out the emotions. Even if you never really liked them.

The sheriff touched the back of my hand, bringing my attention back to him. He must have guessed my answer by my reluctance to give it. But he was still waiting.

"I think it could. But again, not having much in the way of magic myself, Opal would be the one to ask."

He nodded. "My thoughts exactly. You headed back to the farmhouse now?"

Where else would I go? Then I remembered that I'd have to pass the Flour Shop on the way. Maybe my small betrayal would go a little better with Opal if I got her a raspberry delight.

"After a quick stop off to get donuts and coffee, yes."

His hand reached up and ruffled through his hair. It must be a family trait, as Opie did that all the time. Or maybe he was just mimicking his dad. He could do worse. His dad was a good man.

He blew out a breath and dug out his wallet, handing me a ten-dollar bill. "Don't suppose you'd do me a couple of favors? Like pick me up a tall black coffee and a plain glazed donut while you're there?"

I took the money and shoved it in my shirt pocket. "I can do that. What's the second favor?" As if I didn't already know.

"Call your aunt and let her know I'm coming for coffee, donuts, and a couple of questions."

Chapter 5

The call wasn't a pleasant one to make, but Aunt Opal deserved the warning. Especially as the morning after a full moon was the one morning each month that she allowed herself to fully sleep in. The shop wasn't open until noon those days.

I briefly filled her in on what I knew, which wasn't much, and told her I was stopping by to get donuts and coffee and would be there as soon as I could. Not that she needed me there, but still. I was family, and I wanted to hear what was being said. Just as much for myself as for Opal.

The sheriff's car was already sitting behind our house when I got there. I parked beside it—Opal's designated parking spot for my car, out of sight—and grabbed the purchased breakfast and ran in. I couldn't have missed much. At least I hoped not.

The door was standing open into Opal's domain, so I went in. I would have knocked on the doorjamb to let them know I was there, but my hands were kind of full. They'd just have to forgive me for the interruption. After all, they both knew I was coming.

Opal looked up when I entered her sitting room, then her eyes went to the bag in my hand. "I'm really hoping they had my donuts."

"They did. I got you two Raspberry Delights and four plain glazed for the sheriff and me to share." I sat the drink container down on her coffee table. I'd had the shop label the cups so there wouldn't be any confusion over which belonged to whom.

I sat down on the remaining easy chair and grabbed a donut and my latte. The sheriff gave me a look, but I wasn't budging until he told me I had to. There was such a thing as family solidarity.

It didn't take long.

"I think you need to take your latte and donuts upstairs," he said, his voice much more serious than usual. He was using his officer of the law tone, which was worrisome. "But I'd appreciate it if you stuck around for a bit. I'll want to talk with you after I'm done talking with Opal."

Oh, joy. I shrugged like it didn't matter, then picked another donut out of the bag and left the room. At the top of the stairs, I turned left instead of right. Ruby and I never locked the doors into our personal space from the inside of the house, unless we had company and didn't want to be disturbed. Read that as we were making out with a fellow. That hadn't been the case for either of us for quite a while and was part of the reason Ruby was on this stupid singles' retreat. She thought maybe Opal was right, and it was time to settle down.

Truthfully, Opal couldn't care less if Ruby ever settled down. I mean, Opal never had. Not really. She had never even come close to marriage as far as I knew. In fact, learning yesterday about her and George Hill was the first clue I had that she'd ever even dated. Although she gave birth to Ruby, so she'd had to have had at least one man in her life at some point.

My mind was racing along all the different tracks it could take. It did that sometimes to distract itself from the serious parts of my life I wanted so desperately to avoid. But there was no avoiding this.

Once in Ruby's sitting room, I opened the air vent leading down to Opal's. We had discovered long ago, that if we opened that vent, we could hear everything being said below. Came in very handy for eavesdropping.

"You were here all morning after your meeting and altercation with Valerie Kimble?"

"When I think of altercations, sheriff, I think of punches being thrown. Our argument didn't get physical. The only things being thrown were words. But to answer your question, yes, I was here all morning."

There was a pause, and I could imagine Sheriff Taylor going through the motions of making a note in a small notebook. Unfortunately, I didn't have a way to confirm his actions. I could hear, but not see.

"Okay, so it didn't get physical. That's good." Another, shorter pause. "Did it get magical?"

Opal hesitated just long enough to let my heart drop into my stomach. She had done something magical. Crap on toast, what had she done?

"The woman took my donut."

I closed my eyes. This was so not good.

"And... for that she had to die?"

"Don't be ridiculous, sheriff. I wouldn't kill anyone over that. So, if you are asking me if I sent a death spell over to Val, the answer would be no. I did no such thing. We argued, she took my blasted donut, and she went home. Still one hundred percent alive. I have absolutely no idea of what happened to her after that."

I held my breath, waiting for Sheriff Taylor to ask the follow-up question that was on my tongue. "What spell did you throw at her?" But he didn't. He knew our family and, maybe more importantly, Opie was close to us. Unless proven otherwise, or sufficient evidence appeared to make him question our words, he would believe what we said. He trusted his son's judgment in friends. That said a lot about both of them.

"Okay then, I think we're through for now." There were sounds of him getting up. I glanced at the door to Ruby's and hesitated. I didn't want to miss any last questions he might ask, but I also didn't want to be seen going from Ruby's apartment to mine. Once he stepped out Opal's door at the bottom of the steps, my crossing would be visible.

I left. I'd barely made it into my bedroom and was working on a quick making of my bed when the knock came on my door. When I opened it and the sheriff saw my bed sitting there plain as day, he blushed.

"Sorry, sheriff. Most of my company comes from the outside stairs. That entrance leads into my sitting room." This one was for family, but I didn't need to say that.

I led him through to the safer part of the apartment so that his facial coloring could go back to normal. Once we were both sitting on my comfy couch nursing our hot drinks, the questioning began.

"If you don't mind, I'd like you to tell me exactly what happened last night at that meeting. We have an eyewitness that says it got pretty heated. I'd like to know why."

There was a brief pause as I considered how best to word my story. There wasn't any way I was going to lie to Sheriff Taylor. And I knew that Opal wouldn't want that, anyway. We were honest witches, dang it.

"Well, I'll admit that it surprised me when Opal invited Val and her gang to join us for the night to begin with. They've never been the best of friends. Especially now since Opal is going up against her for that town council seat. But she did." I glanced over at him. "If she hadn't, it would have just been the two of us dancing around that fire. That would have been kind of sad."

He grinned. "Not to some people I know, but I get your point. Go on."

I took a deep breath. "Full moon meetings are special. At least they are to us. But Val brought a non-witch guest along with her coven, Tommy Hill."

His eyes widened. "Valerie Kimble brought Fat Geek to your coven meeting? A skyclad meeting? Oh, Opie is not going to be happy about that."

That confused me for a minute. Why would Opie care? Then it hit me. He'd be thinking that Tommy was taking advantage of the situation just to see me naked. That was so not the case.

"Tommy didn't know it was a joint meeting until it was too late for him to back out." I could see the sheriff was doubtful on that point. So be it. I don't know why, but I believed Tommy. "And when he saw the trouble that his being there caused, he left. Voluntarily, and of his own accord." That had to mean something.

Sheriff Taylor chuckled. "Okay, so Tommy didn't do anything wrong. I hear you. But I'm betting that Opal didn't take too kindly to him being there at all."

"No, she didn't." Then I took a deep breath and told him everything, including about the final straw—the taking of the donut.

"Opal really loves those things, doesn't she?"

I nodded. "And they only had the one, so Val knew exactly what she was doing when she did it."

The sheriff sobered. "Do you think Opal would have retaliated over the whole evening's turnout? Sounds like just about enough to push her over the edge."

What did he want me to say? That the first person I thought of when I learned about Val's death was Opal? My aunt and I have our differences, but I'm a lot more loyal than that.

"I'm not going to say that Opal wasn't mad as an old wet hen, because she was. But killing someone over it? No way." For what it's worth I believed every word I said. The sheriff must have been able to tell that because he shut his notebook and stood up. The interview was obviously over.

"Well, if there is anything else you can remember that might help us, be sure to call me, okay?"

"I will. I promise." I paused as we walked toward the outside entrance. No way was I taking him through my bedroom again. "Do you really think someone killed her?" Personally, I was still hoping for a heart attack or something.

He shrugged. "Until we get the coroner's report, we won't know for sure. That means I have to be ready with all the information I can gather in case he comes back with a suspicious death ruling."

I could understand that. He was good at his job. I'd expect nothing less from him. I walked him out to the top of the outside staircase and then watched him as he finished walking to his car. He'd parked out back, and now my car was sitting right beside his. His laughter filtered up to me as he shook his head and climbed into his car. Once he was gone, I went back inside, through my apartment, and back down the stairs to Opal's.

It was time for us to have a talk.

Chapter 6

"What did you do to Val?" Opal wasn't much of one for small talk, so I was just taking my cue from her.

She looked at me for a minute, then turned away. At least she wasn't going to belittle my intelligence by saying she'd done nothing. She might not say a word. That would be totally in keeping with her personality. You can't call it lying if she says nothing, right?

When I had entered, she had been watching the sheriff leave from her picture window facing the road. I was kind of shocked when I saw her deflate right before my eyes and sink onto the couch. Opal was by far the strongest woman I had ever known, and right now she just looked spent.

It was enough to really have me worried.

"I'm going to guess that you heard what I told the sheriff?"

She knew the house better than I did. Stood to reason that she'd know about the ventilation intercom system. No sense in denying it.

"I did. You said that you didn't throw a death spell her way. But he failed to ask the all-important question. What spell did you throw?"

"What time is it?"

What? I glanced at my watch. "Nine o'clock. But what does that have to do with anything?"

"I need a drink, but it's far too early to start drinking. If it was closer to noon, I wouldn't feel so bad about making a onetime exception."

She was stalling. This wasn't good at all. There was something she didn't want to tell me. Worst of all, I could tell she was worried. It was faint, and probably not apparent to anyone who hadn't seen her every single day for their entire life, but it was there.

I waited. My question was still hanging out there, and I didn't intend to go anywhere until she'd answered it.

When she saw I wasn't budging from my self-imposed mission, she relented. Her head was resting on the back of the sofa and her eyes were closed when she started. "It's times like these that I really miss your mother, you know. She always knew what to do when times got rough."

Mom? Really? I'd always thought Mom was just like me in that regard. Opal and Ruby were the two the town really respected. Mom and I were kind of like their sidekicks. But maybe now that was really just me.

"And to answer your question, I threw a harmless karma spell her way. Nothing that would break the witches' creed at all, as it wouldn't be me deciding her punishment, but the universe itself."

I swallowed. We both knew what kind of person Val Kimble was. It was entirely possible that the universe had decided that Valerie Kimble should die. And, in the end, it would have been Opal's spell that maybe helped it along.

"When did you cast it?"

"Right before I turned in this morning. About three or so." She pinched the bridge of her nose. "Where is your mom now? Do you think it's too early to call her?"

"I think she'd be fine with a call from you anytime, Opal. But I haven't been able to reach her for days. Knowing Mom, she's lost her phone again." I paused. "I think we should call Ruby too."

"No! I want a grandchild while I'm still young enough to enjoy them. As she certainly wasn't meeting her match here in Wind's Crossing, this retreat is her best shot at meeting someone suitable."

"Don't you think that should take a back burner to what's going on right now? We need to find out exactly what happened to Val." I didn't want to come right out and say it, but she knew what I meant. We needed all the magic we could get. As I didn't have much to contribute, and Mom was out of the country, that meant Ruby and Opal. At least I could help fill out the trinity of numbers, but that was about the extent of my worthwhile contribution.

Opal rallied. "And we will. If the police don't beat us to it." Her eyes bore into mine. "But Ruby stays where she is. It's only two more days. I've got this. Now go back upstairs and get back to bed. That's where I'm going after letting the animals back out of my bedroom."

Yeah, it was hard talking with anyone, let alone a lawman, with Bridget and Yorkie Doodle in the room. I had been wondering what she'd done with them.

"A tired witch doesn't think properly. It's entirely possible the Goddess will solve all of this kerfuffle while we sleep."

Oh, it was possible but highly unlikely.

***

When my alarm went off two hours later, I was filled with resolve. I was going to do what I should have done years ago. Get a familiar and find my magic. I could feel the stupid power inside me at times like this. On the off chance that Opal was right and having a familiar could help me tap into it, I needed to bite the dang bullet and do it. Surely, I could learn to handle the allergies, right?

Ruby's dog, Yorkie Doodle, didn't bother me too bad, as long as I wasn't in prolonged contact with him. But then, a dog was fine for a powerful witch. I needed something more.

I needed a cat. There was a reason they were the most popular animal for witches' familiars. Even if my entire family had been nice enough to not go that route in deference to me. Ruby had Yorkie Doodle, my mom had Komo the bearded dragon, and Aunt Opal had Bridget the Macaw.

Now, after all their generosity to me in choosing familiars, I was going to break the chain. I loaded up on water and took another couple of bottles with me. Then I popped an allergy tablet and headed out of town.

Wind's Crossing had a local animal shelter, but I didn't want to go there. They knew us Ravenswinds there and weren't all that fond of handing out animals to witches. For the life of me, I couldn't understand why. Familiars had the best life of any animals on earth. We take very good care of them. Well, witches in general do, and I planned to do my part too.

Shoot, I might have to section off a part of our balcony and give the new kitty its very own space. I'd have to remember to ask Opal if I had to be in the same room as my cat in order to feed power through him. That would be kind of important to know.

My goal wasn't even the next town over or the town after that. I was trying to make lemonade out of the lemons here. I was finally taking my new baby for a decent spin. Our town was about thirty-five miles north of the Indiana state line. That was my objective. Crossing that line.

I'd done some research online, and there was a likely looking no-kill shelter a few miles past that invisible border. According to their website, they were overstocked on cats at the moment and pretty desperate to adopt them out. That meant they had cut their normal adoption fee in half. For an unemployed witch working side gigs, that was an important consideration.

I downed another bottle of water and took another half of an allergy pill. I know that was above the recommended dose, but I was hoping it would be enough to do the trick. The water was to help fight the dehydration that came with the antihistamine. My life could never be a simple one.

Steeling myself for the sneezing I knew would come, I climbed out of my car and went in. Just before I got to the door, I reached into my purse and pulled out the hospital type face mask.

When I approached the desk, the receptionist stepped back a few steps, giving me an odd look. Yeah, bet they didn't get too many red-headed witches wearing face masks here.

I smiled at her before I realized she most likely couldn't tell I was even smiling. I tried to put the smile into my voice.

"Don't worry, I'm not contagious or anything." I made a face, making sure to use parts of it that she could see. "I just had surgery, and the doctors want me to wear this stupid thing every time I go outside for another whole week. Can you believe it?"

Her shoulders returned to normal, and her eyes left the can of Lysol that was sitting on the shelf behind the desk. I was guessing she was a bit of a germophobe. Not that I blamed her. Germs were even nastier little critters than cats.

"How can I help you today? Are you looking to adopt? I'm afraid we aren't taking any more cats at this time." She shrugged. "There's only so much room here, I'm afraid."

"Well, I'm hoping to help with that. I'd love to adopt a new kitty. I just lost my old one a month ago, and I think it's time to move on. I really miss having a little fur baby around." Opal may have a problem with lying, but in situations like this, it seemed to come second nature to me.

Now the woman was all smiles. "Oh, that's wonderful news! Well, not the losing your fur baby part, but you know what I mean. Choosing a new kitty is always so exciting! Follow me, I'll take you to our cat enclosure."

I took a deep breath and followed as instructed. When I saw the cat enclosure, as she called it, I could have laughed in relief. Making the drive had definitely been worth it. The entire enclosure was surrounded by glass, a wonderful, allergy containing design if ever there was one. The whole idea was to look in and pick out one or two likely pet mates and they'd bring them out for you. Then you could get to know them a little one on one in a side room made just for that.

It was the perfect setup. That didn't mean, however, that there wasn't still plenty of cat dander floating in the air. Cats still had to pass through the open halls occasionally.

I sneezed and a black cat sitting by the window looked up at me, and I could have sworn he laughed. I wasn't sure if he was laughing at my sneeze or at the stupid mask I was wearing, but I know a snickering cat when I see one. Even if it was my first.

"Did he just laugh at me?"

The lady gave me a funny look. "Cats don't really laugh, you know. He probably has a hairball. He's new here and hasn't been fully treated for everything yet. Probably ate something before coming in that bothered him."

I looked into his eyes, and he stared back into mine. I didn't know cats could roll their eyes, but this one could.

"He's the one I want." I pointed to him just to be sure we were all on the same page. The cat's eyes widened as if in surprise. Too bad, kitty cat, you're the one. Don't worry, you'll have a good life and much longer than any other cat here. Familiars had extremely long life spans. Something about the magic flowing through them on a daily basis. Well, that and the bond to their witch. Both helped, I'm sure.

"Oh, I'm afraid he isn't nearly ready for adoption. As I said, he's new and hasn't been fully treated yet. We'll have to get him neutered and let him recover from that before we could even think about adoption."

If I thought the cat's eyes had widened before, they were now comically so. That cat seemed to understand exactly what she had said. Whoever said cats didn't have facial expressions were dead wrong. This one was the Clint Eastwood of cats. Rugged, sleek, and easy to read.

"There's another black cat over there. It's about a year old and all up to date on shots and everything. She would probably work much better for you."

The laughing cat wasn't laughing anymore. Now his eyes were a bit on the pleading side.

Don't worry, buddy, I thought. I've got your back. And just think how very grateful he'd be to me for saving him. Super smart and grateful. That had to be a great combination for a familiar.

Now if I could just get lucky and have him be hypoallergenic too, I'd have it made.

The lady was disappointed that she couldn't talk me into one of the other three dozen cats they had, but my mind was made up. There was only one cat for me, and that was Mr. Smartypants. I mean, come on, how many cats were that smart? Plus, I figured the attitude was a good match for me. We should get along just fine. At least I would understand him. Even without the bond, he was pretty easy to read.

I gave them a fake name and phone number and told her to call me when he was ready for adoption. Not that he'd be there by then.

No. I was breaking him out.

And as he was scheduled for his vet visit first thing in the morning, it had to be tonight.

Goddess help me.

Chapter 7

On the way home to get a few things, I realized I had a whole afternoon to kill. Breaking and entering was a job best done after dark. And, of course, preferably after all the workers had left for the day.

I was taking a big risk, and once we were bonded, I would be sure he understood that. He would bloody well owe me. Just the way I wanted it.

As I drove, my mind wandered back to the situation with Valerie's death. I was still hoping it would turn out to be natural causes, but I wasn't holding my breath on that being the case. We'd have been home free if only Opal hadn't cast that karma spell. But hey, for once it wasn't me that had made the stupid rookie-type mistake.

And, now that I thought about it, if I could somehow prove Opal wasn't at fault, she would owe me. That had never happened before. It was always her pulling my rear from the fire, not the other way around.

That brought a smile to my face. Then there was the added bonus of this being a dry run for my upcoming career as a private detective. A practice case. Thinking of it that way helped too.

I could so do this.

By the time I made it back to Wind's Crossing, I knew just where to go first. Misty Rhodes' house. Misty worked from home as a virtual personal assistant. I wasn't sure how that worked, but it seemed to pay her bills, and it let her be home with her kids before and after school too. If I remembered right, they were in first and third grades. One was seven, and the other was nine.

The good news was that meant that right now, Misty should be home alone. Perfect for a little chat. The sheriff had known about the run in at the coven meeting, and I wanted to know how. It had only happened a few hours before they found Val's body. Misty lived on the other side of town, but somehow, I just knew in my gut that she had been the one to blab about it. The question I wanted answered most of all, though, was how did she know Val was dead?

I parked on the street in front of her house and walked up to the door. The virtual job might be enough to keep them all fed and the lights on, but it didn't look like there was much left over for home maintenance. The house could definitely do with a paint job. One shutter on a front window was hanging askew, and another was totally missing.

When she pulled the curtain back and saw me standing there, she didn't look happy. But she opened the door, probably because she could tell I'd seen her. I had waved to let her know.

"I'm guessing you want to know about Val too, right? Well, I can save you some time. I don't know anything." The door started shutting, and I put my foot out to stop it.

"I just want to ask you a couple of questions, okay? I thought maybe we could help each other out."

She took a deep breath and opened the door back but didn't invite me in. She stood in the threshold barring my path. "So ask your questions already. I've got work to get done before my little demons get home."

"Do you know anyone that might have been on the outs with Valerie? Other than Opal, I mean."

Misty shrugged. "She wasn't the nicest of people, you know. There were a lot of folks who really didn't like her." She paused. "Maybe she did something on the town council that ticked someone off…" Her voice trailed off even as her eyes widened.

"What?" I knew that look. She'd thought of something. Something big.

She swallowed and looked down at her arm only to find she wasn't wearing a watch. "Look, I really don't think that's it after all. I mean the only person I know that was mad enough at Val to do something to her is Opal. Sorry, but that's the truth. Now, I have work to do."

I caught the door again. "Just one more question. Other than Tommy Hill, that started everything, did you see anyone at the meeting last night that shouldn't have been there? Someone out of place or watching?"

Misty's eyes closed for a few seconds. When they reopened, she looked thoughtful. "Well, you know I had to leave early to come back and relieve the sitter. On my way down the road from your house, Naomi Hill passed me in that big blue Buick of hers. At first, I thought it was odd with how late it was and all, but then I realized she was most likely chasing down her husband George. She tries to keep him on a tight leash on full moon nights, but maybe he broke free and she was out to retrieve him? Either way, she's the only one I saw on the road until I reached town." She gave me a pointed look. "Now will you please go away and let me earn my living?"

"Sure, and sorry to have bothered…" I was talking to a closed door.

When I turned to walk back to my car, I found an old woman walking her dog on the sidewalk. She stared at me in distaste. "Is this your car?"

"Yes, but it came with the paint job. I'm planning to get it painted soon."

"Well, you'd better. This is public obscenity. Something should be done about it." Then she tilted her head up and walked off.

Yeah, those decals I ordered couldn't get here fast enough.

***

After getting home, I debated my next step. Even if Opal had practically forbidden it, I really thought Ruby had a right to know what was going on here. Especially as it involved her mom. The fact that Ruby's magic would make breaking into the shelter so much easier was purely irrelevant. Or so I kept telling myself.

She answered on the third ring.

"Hey, Amie what's shaking?"

"Where do I start? First, though, are you sitting down? I think you need to be sitting down for this." I paused. "I'm not interrupting anything, am I?" As it was only the middle of the day, I hoped that was the case. How embarrassing would it be to call in the middle of a make out session?

Her voice sobered. "Is Mom okay? For that matter, are you okay?"

"Still healthy and no bones broken, so yeah, mostly okay. It's just that, well, there's been a bit of an incident here."

I heard her groan through the phone. "Did you and Mom get into it again?"

Why does everyone assume that? I know Opal and I are very different people, but we were actually on the same side on this one. It kind of felt nice. Totally weird, but nice.

"Nothing like that. You know last night was the full moon." I didn't make it a question. All witches know when the moon is full, it's kind of built into our internal wiring. "Well, Opal invited the Windsong Coven to join us."

She gasped. "You're kidding! Valerie finally got what she wanted?"

"Well, not exactly. Val's dead."

Silence.

"Ruby, are you there?"

"I'm here. It's just… Mom's involved, isn't she? Oh Goddess, please tell me Mom didn't kill her."

Now it was my turn to be quiet. How do you tell someone that might not be the case at all? Opal's spell might have been the catalyst for whatever had happened to Valerie. And now that I really thought about it, that could be the case even if they ruled her death as natural. The Goddess could give heart attacks and strokes all day long if she wanted to. And Valerie had a lot of bad karma built into her history here on earth.

"Okay, walk me through it. Start from the beginning and don't leave anything out."

I did. It took a while, but I caught her up as quickly as I could.

"So, all Mom did was throw a karma spell, right? She didn't strangle her with her bare hands or anything? No trace evidence that could be found on the body?"

"Well…"

"Besides the spell mark, I mean. Of course, she's gonna have that. But the cops wouldn't know what it was, so we don't have to worry there. And you can be Opal's alibi that she didn't leave the house, right?"

"I'm an alibi for sure, for whatever good a family alibi does. But about the cops knowing thing…"

"Oh, my Goddess. You've told Opie about the spell mark, haven't you?"

"Not recently, but yeah, a while back. In his line of work, I really thought he should know."

She hesitated. "Okay, I'll give you that one. I just wish his first instance of finding one wouldn't be on this particular case."

"Me too."

"How's Mom holding up?"

We talked for a few more minutes, with me bouncing ideas off her, then I turned to the second reason for my call. The much more personal one.

"So have you found a mate yet?"

Silence again. That didn't bode well. Or maybe it did for me. If she hadn't found anyone, maybe she would be free tonight. The retreat was in Chicago, so she could get here in just a few hours if she left now.

"If I tell you something, do you swear on the moon you won't spill it to Mom?"

I leaned back into my chair. This was going to be good. "Of course."

"I'm not at the retreat right now. I'm at Rose's."

Ruby's friend Rose just lived one town away. I'd passed by her bloody house on my way to Indiana.

"Spill it."

"Well, the first night at the retreat, they did this speed dating kind of thing. I met what I thought was a really cool guy, you know? Tall, handsome, and actually interesting for a change. He's an architect, and right now he's working on a big chapel or something. So intelligent too. The perfect trifecta in a man, right?"

"What happened?"

"Well, we were getting along so well, and our time was running out, so I cast a little truth spell and asked him one final question."

"Oh dear, what did you ask?"

"A very simple question. 'What's the one thing you most don't want me to know about you?' You're not going to believe his answer."

"Let me guess. He's a serial killer? He lives in his mom's basement? He really works at the McDonald's drive-through?" Although, in my mind, the last two weren't all that bad. But Ruby's standards are much higher than mine are.

"Nope, none of the above. The guy was married. As it turns out, being single isn't actually a requirement for attending a singles' retreat."

I winched. "Ouch." Then I paused. "Karma spell?"

She giggled. "Much worse. I got hold of his phone when he wasn't looking and sent a few pictures of him at the dating tables to his wife. If I was his wife, I know I'd want to know where he was."

"Well, yeah. Gives her time to get a jump on the divorce proceedings."

"Exactly."

I took a deep breath. It was now or never. "So you're free to help me with a little project tonight?"

She was getting great at those short silences. "That depends on the project."

"I'm getting a familiar. And don't laugh, but it's a cat—they're the strongest from everything I've read, and I need all the magical strength I can get." I waited for her laughter to subside. People always laugh, even when you tell them not to. Hardwired, I guess. Once she settled down, I told her the problem.

"So you have to get him out tonight or they will alter him?"

"Yup. And if you could have seen the look in his eyes, you'd know he understood every single word we said. He knows what's coming." I paused. "And he laughed at me when I sneezed."

"Cats don't laugh, silly."

"Yeah, well, this one did." I was sticking by it. My future familiar might have an attitude problem, but he was special in his own right. Somehow, I just knew we were meant for each other.

After the call, I forced down another bottle of water and climbed back in bed. The allergy pills were kicking my behind, but I kept telling myself I'd get used to them, eventually. I just hoped double dosing did the trick. There was no turning back now.

Right before I fell asleep, I sent a mental message to my future familiar.

Don't worry, buddy. I'm coming for ya.

Chapter 8

Ruby had been adamant about not coming home yet. The retreat lasted until the end of the day tomorrow, and she was really hoping to keep the fact that she'd left that first night a secret just between the two of us. As long as Opal didn't ask me outright, I should be good to keep it.

Here's the thing. I'm pretty sure that Opal spelled us when we were just babies. Or maybe she did it once we began to talk. Either way, I'm fairly certain the spell took place. I've never been able to lie to Opal. Or my mom, for that matter. Anyone else, no problem, I can stretch the truth just as far as I want to. With them, I cannot lie. Just like George Washington and the apple tree legend. My plan was to keep out of her sight until Ruby made it home. Then whatever story Ruby told, I'd just nod and go along with it.

I'd have to ask Ruby to help me break the spell. It had become very obvious to me that the spell no longer worked on her. If she could break it on herself, surely she could do the same for me. But that was for another time and place. Right now, I had a mission to prepare for.

It took a few minutes to gather all the ingredients that Ruby had asked for and find her personal spell book. Not that she'd keep it there after today. I really don't know why she bothers to hide it, as she has a strong spell binding it to open only for her. Still, I guess one could destroy it. The very thought made me shiver. All those hours of experimenting and work would be wasted if the book were gone. Maybe I understood why she would hide it after all.

I shoved everything in my backpack and headed out. The drive seemed much longer tonight than it had earlier. Part of that was the fact that twilight was looming, but another part was knowing what came at the end.

The sad thing is, I wasn't really worried about the whole breaking and entering part. I was, however, scared to death at the thought of having a familiar. It was something I'd put off for a very long time.

Even apart from the sneezing fits, there was an underlying worry. What if having a familiar made absolutely no difference in my magical ability? I mean, I'd be happy to just be able to light a candle with magic. I'm not asking for the kind of power Opal or Mom—even Ruby—has. Just... something. A little magic would mean a lot to me. Especially after a lifetime of not having any at all.

Opal's thought was that a familiar might do the trick. Help me harness my power and strengthen the trickle of magic in me. At this point, I was terrified that she would turn out to be wrong.

The worst thing that could happen? I'd be a sneezing, red-nosed un-magical cat owner. I could live with that.

I hoped.

The shelter was dark when I pulled in behind the building. Luckily, it wasn't directly in town. Pretty secluded, actually, which worked well for our purposes. Ruby's rental car was already there, and she was sitting on the hood staring at the building.

"Did you bring everything I told you to?" Her gaze never left the structure in front of her.

"Yup. It's all in my backpack."

"Good." But still, she didn't move.

"Can I ask what you're doing?"

She held up one finger, then gave a short nod and hopped off the hood. "I was just checking to make sure there wasn't anyone inside."

I looked from the building to her. Part of me wanted to ask if she could really do that, but it was Ruby. She wouldn't have said it if she hadn't already done it. Dang, but I wanted a piece of that kind of magic. Just think how handy it would come in for a detective.

Ruby took the backpack and rummaged through it, pulling out two small bags of herbs and mixing a pinch of each in the palm of her right hand. Then she closed her eyes and chanted a few words, ending the chant with one final stir of the herbs.

"Okay, I'm ready. Back door?"

"Probably for the best. I didn't see any cameras when I was here earlier, but it doesn't hurt to stay out of sight from the road."

She nodded and headed toward it. I followed. Within seconds of reaching it, Ruby reached down and opened it.

The door led into a back room filled with a row of cages. In the third cage to the right was my new best friend. He must have been the only one going to the vet because all the other cages were empty. I know I was getting ahead of myself, but I was feeling really hopeful about this.

But something was wrong with him. He tried to stand up, but he listed to one side and ended up leaning against the cage. His eyes, however, locked onto mine. They were still pleading.

"Is he sick?" Ruby gave him a critical look. "You do know they have others to choose from, right?"

I just looked at her. Like we weren't at a blooming animal shelter filled with abandoned animals. "You sound just like the lady who tried to help me today." I bent down and met him on eye to eye level. There was definitely a connection between us.

Finally, I realized that Ruby was staring at me. "What?"

"I think you're right. He's the one for sure."

Okay, I knew I felt that way, but what had convinced Ruby when only seconds ago she'd been suggesting another animal?

"Why do you say that?"

"You're eyeball to eyeball with a cat, and you aren't sneezing your fool head off. I'd say that was a really good sign."

"Well, I have taken a double dose of allergy medication today."

Ruby chuckled. "And has that ever worked this well before?"

She had a point. Bending down, I took a closer look at my new fur mate. "So fellow, you ready to break outta here?"

He nodded slowly, then fell over and started softly snoring. I heard Ruby suck in a breath beside me. "Are you totally sure he isn't already somebody's familiar? Cats just aren't this smart."

I flashed her a smile. "Well, this one is, and he's going to be mine after tonight." I paused. "If he is already bound to another witch, it won't let me do the spell, right?"

Her teeth caught her bottom lip in her traditional thinking pose. "That sounds right, but I'll double-check before we do the binding spell." She bent down for a closer look. "Is he okay though? I really don't want you taking him home if he's sick. I don't want him passing the bug to Yorkie Doodle."

"He was fine today. I think they just gave him some kind of drug to get him ready for tomorrow."

"Ah, yes, that makes sense." She looked around. "So how do we do this? You know if we just take him, they'll know there was a break in, right?"

Another fine point. Thinking fast, I pointed out into the main building. "What if we grab another black cat and stuff him in the cage?" We'd brought Yorkie Doodle's traveling suite with us, so we didn't need theirs.

"That might work, but all of them are fixed, right? Won't they be able to tell the difference?"

"Well, hopefully. I'd hate to think they'd operate on the same cat twice, but I'm thinking they'd believe it was just an error." I fingered the little metal tag on his collar. "Especially if we switched their tags. The other cat would just be missing then." And I hadn't been interested in that one, so hopefully, they wouldn't connect me to the switcheroo.

I stepped out into the main building and immediately sneezed. Ruby laughed, but at least my new smart-alec cat slept through it.

"So much for the allergy medicine. You stay here. I'll go grab another cat."

Ruby went through the door and closed it behind her. Once me and Blackie were alone, the sneezing wound down. I stared at him in awe. Had I really found a cat I wasn't allergic to? How awesome would that be?

The door reopened and Ruby motioned for me to take my new cat and get out. It wasn't fast enough. The sneezing started again. I slipped the collar off him and handed it to Ruby and then hustled out of there. In less than two minutes she joined me outside.

"I took an extra step and cast a sleeping spell on the other cat. With any luck, it will look like he was drugged too."

"Are you coming home with me?"

She laughed. "And have to explain to Mom why I'm home early? No thanks, I know how much this retreat cost her. I really don't want the lectures for weeks on end. Besides, it isn't like it was my fault it didn't work out, now is it?"

"Nope, in my eyes you did your part." I shoved the carrier into the back seat and turned back to Ruby. Part of me was really wishing she was coming home now. I could use her help. My work wasn't nearly done yet.

"You can do the spell." She always could read me. "Just follow the directions in my spell book to the letter. It's an easy one, I promise. Even the plain everyday human witches can do it. You can too."

I sure hoped she was right. But I wasn't feeling all warm and fuzzy about it.

Finally, she blew out a breath. "Okay, how's about this. We go to the park I passed on the way here, we make a circle, and we do this thing right now."

My eyes caught hers. "Do we have everything we need?"

More lip chewing, but eventually, she nodded. "Enough to get the job done. It really is an easy spell, but this way I can walk you through it and make sure nothing goes wrong." She paused. "And for the record, I'm not doubting your ability to do this. But with the intelligence of this cat... well, I just think maybe I should watch."

I couldn't agree more. There was far too much riding on doing this right to risk letting me do the thing on my own. I mean, come on, where on earth was I going to find another cat like this one?

Chapter 9

It was just after eleven o'clock and I was following Ruby's rental to the park when my cell phone whistled. That was the ringtone that alerted me that Opie was calling.

Goddess help me, but my first thought was that he knew where we were and exactly what we had just done. He could read me every bit as well as Ruby, but surely, not from miles away. After all, he wasn't a witch. Not yet, anyway. It was something he'd been considering, but he hadn't pulled that particular trigger yet.

I reached over and swiped the screen, then pushed the button for speakerphone.

"Hey, Opie, what's up?" I mean something had to be up for him to be calling this late. He was an early to bed kind of guy.

"Where are you?"

No preamble. Uh-oh. "I met Ruby to let her in on what was going on. Wasn't something I wanted to do over the phone." Kind of sort of the truth, at least in part.

"Are you with her now? Somewhere close?"

"Not really close, we're on our way to a park to do a mini meeting. There's a spell Ruby is wanting to try out." This time nothing but the truth. This was too easy.

There was a brief moment of silence. "Okay, I really didn't want to do this over the phone, but here it goes anyway. Would you like to tell me why Opal's spell mark is on Valerie Kimble?"

Crap, not only had he remembered, he'd found it. That was bad. It meant the spell had taken effect before she'd died. Thus, it could have been the reason she died. But I couldn't really say that, could I? At this point, the autopsy was kind of a moot point. I mean, magic can give a person a heart attack if the witch welding it is powerful enough. We both knew Opal had more than enough power for that type of spell.

"She took her donut, for Goddess' sake, Opie. You think Opal would let that slide after what went down that night? No way. But it wasn't a death spell. Opal told me so, and your father too, and you know Opal doesn't lie."

More silence.

"Okay for now. But only because we should have the coroner's report by the morning. Once I see what's in it, we'll likely be having another little talk. In person."

"Look forward to it." Ruby's car flashed its right turn signal. We must be close to the park. "Well, it looks like we're here. Did you need anything else tonight?"

"No. Just… be careful out there, okay? You don't have all that much experience driving. I don't like that you're that far from home after dark so soon after getting your car."

"I'm a good driver." A squirrel ran down a tree next to the road, and I swerved, certain it was going to dart in front of me. Good thing Opie didn't see that. "See you soon."

I hung up just as I was parking next to Ruby. She was already out of her car and waiting, looking over the small park.

Joining her, I gave her an Opie update. She just shook her head.

"As soon as you told me he knew what to look for, I knew he'd find it. He's good at what he does. But we'll deal with that once we find out what killed her. Right now, we have magic to do."

And nothing ever got between Ruby and a spell casting. Not even a possible unsolved murder.

"There." She pointed to a path that ran between the trees at the edge of the park. "We'll walk down the path until we find a place big enough to cast a circle. That way, we'll be out of sight. We don't want interruptions for this."

I grabbed Blackie—I would have to come up with a name for him soon—and we headed into the woods. Several yards in, there was a small clearing off to the side that Ruby deemed perfect for our needs.

"Set him down in the middle of this spot, while I get the circle ready." She peered into his cage. "Is he really asleep, you think or just faking it? We don't want him running off before we get him bound."

"Should we keep him in the kennel?"

She hesitated, but then shook her head. "Too risky. Remember, you'll be the one doing the actual spell work. We don't need anything in the way between the two of you."

That made sense. While she went about taking care of the circle, I slowly opened the carrier and waited. No movement. I reached in and poked him. Still nothing. I lifted one of his paws and let it go. It fell heavily to the kennel's floor. He was totally out. Not that I liked the idea of him being drugged, but I'd admit it made things a bit easier on us.

Reaching in, I pulled him out into the open. He was a long-haired beauty, and I was shocked at how soft and silky his fur was. I couldn't remember ever touching a cat before. Their fur was so very different from a dog's. Lifting him up I took a deep breath and snuggled my face into his side.

Then I waited. Nothing. Not even a tickle in my nose. This had to be the work of the Goddess. There just wasn't any other explanation I could think of as to why I wasn't, as Ruby had put it, sneezing my fool head off.

"If you're done testing out the whole allergy thing, I'm ready when you are. And I'd like to get to bed sometime soon."

Oh yeah, right, the spell. Sue me, but I'd never gotten to handle a cat before. I was already more than halfway in love with the little guy.

"This won't hurt him, right?"

She smiled at me. "No, it doesn't hurt them. And, for what it's worth, it should be a great thing for him too. He'll be spoiled, and taken good care of, and live for a really long time."

I grinned at her. "And still be able to father children. That has to mean something too, right?"

Ruby laughed. "I think he would agree to that."

Placing him in the center of the circle, I hesitated for a minute watching him. Still no sign of movement. I took the few steps back to stand beside Ruby.

She handed me a piece of paper and then conjured up a light for me to read it by. "Memorize it and whenever you're ready, step into the circle and close it."

The words were simple but powerful. Just what I'd expect from my cousin.

> *I pledge to thee my life and love*
> *Through thick and thin, magic and blood.*
> *Bound to you and you to me,*
> *Forever more, so shall it be.*

When I had it down, I stepped into the circle, closed it quickly, and looked back to Ruby. "What next?"

"Kneel before him and place your hand on his head, then say the words. When you're finished, kiss him." She shrugged. "The spell needs an act of love to take hold."

Sounded okay to me. I gave her a crooked smile. "He's not going to turn into a handsome witch, is he? I mean, not that I'd complain about that." I had about the same luck as Ruby when it came to the masculine sex. That is to say bad. But then my mom wasn't pressuring me to produce a magical heir. At least I had that going for me.

"Don't be silly. This is serious. Are you sure you're ready for this? Please remember that forever is a death do you part kind of thing."

I took a deep breath and glanced down at the sleeping cat. I'd never been able to be around one this close before. It was something I could get used to. In fact, it would be super nice to have a roommate that I didn't have to pick up after or cook for.

"I'm ready."

I followed her instructions to the letter and as my lips touched his furry noggin; the spell caught. To be honest, I had been more than half expecting it not to work. I mean, my magic could fit in a pinkie-sized thimble and still have room left over. But the instant my lips touched him, I could feel the power in me shift into something very… different.

Goddess help me, I couldn't resist trying to pull a little magic through him. The rush was intoxicating.

Right up until Ruby screamed, "Stop!"

I opened my eyes and looked at her. She was staring at me in what looked to be abject terror. What the heck? My first thought was something had happened to the cat, but he was still sleeping peacefully, so I glanced behind the circle to see if the danger lay there.

That was when I noticed my hair. It was dancing. Huh. It didn't usually do that. When Ruby cast a spell or gathered magic, her hair would float around her, but mine didn't stop at floating. Each strand appeared to be in constant motion.

And the weirdness didn't stop there. I noticed an odd sensation in my hands and when I glanced down at them; I caught Ruby's fear. Blue and white electrical arcs were sparking from my fingertips.

Worst of all, I had no idea how to safely release it. I had no spell prepared. I wasn't sure there was a spell to handle this much magic.

I had to struggle to breathe, and it took me a minute to strangle out words. "What do I do, Ruby?"

She was still staring at me, hard. Then she gave a frantic look around the small clearing. Over to one side, there was a tiny sapling, the earth still broken and dark around it from its recent planting.

Speaking slowly, she pointed to the tiny tree. "We are air witches, and as such our magic doesn't work so well on earth spells, like growing things. That should work in our favor. Give me a minute to come up with a spell."

Her lip chewing went into double-time as the electrical charges danced up my hands and into my arms. Who knew what would happen if they reached something important... like my heart.

"Would you mind very much hurrying it up?"

"Okay, walk slowly over to that sapling and say this: Baby tree grow and live, my nurturing magic I freely give. Then touch it lightly and step back quickly."

I nodded, not even able to force out the words to agree to her plan. Stepping out of the circle I was within reach of the tiny tree within seconds. For someone who had desperately wanted magic her entire life, now I was every bit as desperate to get rid of it.

"Baby tree grow and live, my nurturing magic I freely give." I touched the smallest branch at the top of the sapling and took two quick steps back. It wasn't enough.

The earth literally rumbled under my feet, throwing me off balance and down to the ground. I barely kept my head from hitting a large rock. When I got a hold of myself enough to glance back at the tree, I couldn't believe my eyes. The sapling was gone.

At first, I thought I had disintegrated it, then I realized that wasn't the case. Where it had stood there was now a massive oak tree.

I don't know exactly what happened after that, because that's when, for the first time in my life, I fainted.

Chapter 10

When I came to, Opie's worried face was the first thing I saw. Where did he come from? Come to think of it, where was I, anyway?

Then it all came rushing back. The cat, the binding spell, the magic, the oak tree, everything.

Opie handed me a paper sack. "Breathe."

While I was breathing in and out into the sack, I glanced around. I was at Opie's apartment. His bedroom to be exact. Funny, in all the time I'd known him, I don't think I'd ever seen this room before, and yet, I instantly knew that the room was his. Of course, that could have had something to do with the multiple pictures of the three of us scattered around. The one on his nightstand was of just me and him. We looked happy.

Ruby walked in carrying a tray with tea and crackers. "Ah good, you're awake. You owe me. Opie wanted to rush you to the hospital, but I told him you'd be fine."

Maybe. But my head hurt. The hand not holding the bag reached to the back of my head, and I winced. There was a small knot there. Then I remembered that rock. I must not have missed it on my second fall. Good thing my head was closer to the ground for that one.

Finally, I risked taking the bag away, but I kept it close. "What happened?"

Ruby sat down on the bed next to me. "Well, when you passed out, I called Opie. He must have driven like a demon because he got to us in record time. Then we packed up your new familiar and brought you here." She made a face. "You'll have to get your car later. We left a note with it, so hopefully, they won't have it towed."

"Towed?"

"Worry about that later," Opie said, his eyes searching mine. "How are you feeling? I still think we should take you to be checked out. You aren't the fainting type."

Yeah, well, he hadn't been there. Or seen what I'd seen.

I glanced around until I saw his alarm clock. "Has anyone called Opal?" Ruby and I might be twenty-four years old, but that didn't mean we could stay out all night without checking in with the parental units. Right now, that meant Opal, even for me.

Ruby nodded. "Yeah. You're covered there."

Then why wouldn't she meet my eyes? Come to think of it, how had she called Opal without giving away the fact that she was no longer at the retreat?

Too many questions and my head wasn't giving up its right to cause major pain. I laid back on the soft pillow and closed my eyes. At least I was breathing normally now, that was an improvement.

"Where is Blackie?"

"In the backseat of my squad car. My landlord has a very strict no pets policy."

"What if he wakes up and has to go to the bathroom? Don't male cats spray urine?"

"Crap. I'll be right back."

Once he left the room, I turned my gaze to Ruby. "What really happened out there?"

She still looked more than a little scared. "I'm not sure. I mean, as air witches, that spell should have been cut by half. Air magic doesn't work well on earth spells. Or it shouldn't. But if that was only half the spell..." She swallowed. "I'd say you might be the most powerful of all of us."

No blooming way.

"How? You know me. Every single time I've tried to do magic, I've failed. I can't even light a candle, but now I can grow an oak tree in mere seconds?"

"All I can say is that's what happened. How, I don't know. We need Mom's help on this, but Opie's place was closer, and he wanted to stick around until he was sure you were okay."

We heard the apartment door and a few seconds later Opie came in with the carrier and its tiny occupant. "If I lose my living space over this, I want you to know I'm moving in with you."

Wouldn't that be an interesting turn of events? But what I said was, "Sure thing." Then I eyed the small carrier. I really needed to come up with a name for him. But as we would be together for a very long time, I didn't want to rush it. I wanted to make it right.

But some things couldn't wait. "We need to give him something to use as a litter box."

Opie just looked at me. "Do I look like I keep kitty litter around?" Then he paused. "But the kids next door have a sandbox."

It was obvious he was struggling with the concept of actually stealing. Even if it was just a small box full of sand.

"Oh, for the Goddess' sake, I'll get it," Ruby said. "Do you at least have a container we can use?"

He nodded and pulled a shoebox out of his closet. She snatched it out of his hand and left in a huff. We could hear the sliding glass door open out onto the patio and a minute later, she was back with a box half full of sand.

Ruby glared at Opie. "You gonna arrest me?"

He glared back. "Look, don't push me tonight, okay? It's been a rough one and I'm on the edge right now."

Her look softened. "Sorry. I guess I'm a bit edgy too."

"So," Opie drawled dragging the word out. "Are you two going to tell me what happened out there, or is it super-secret witch business?"

I looked to Ruby, and she gave a small shrug. It looked like this was up to me. Stood to reason, as it was kind of my news to tell. And it wasn't like we could keep it from him forever. He was always around. He'd find out sooner rather than later, anyway.

"We were at the park doing a binding spell. Opal's been after me to get a familiar for years now, saying it might help me get in touch with my magic. With everything going on, I decided now was a good time to find out if she was right."

"And you chose a cat?" His eyes flew to the carrier and then back to me. "Wait a minute. Why aren't you sneezing?"

I shook my head, then regretted it. "Somehow, he's special. He doesn't make me sneeze. I'm thinking he must be my destiny." Destiny. There was that word again. Sounded like a good name to me. "Destiny. I think that's what I'll call him."

"Great, your cat has a name," Opie said. "So what happened? Did the binding spell go horribly wrong?"

"No, the binding spell went perfectly," Ruby said. "But then she got impatient and started pulling magic from him before I had a chance to stop her."

Opie's eyes widened. "She has magic now?"

Boy, did I ever.

***

Opie wouldn't agree to let me out of his sight for the night, or really what amounted to the rest of the morning. He had pulled out a cot from his closet and set it up next to the bed. Ruby took the couch.

It was touching that they cared so much. Made me feel good to have people that loved me. Maybe one day, my new cat Destiny would love me too.

When I woke up the next morning, the knot had gone down, and I felt stronger than I ever had. Who knew magic could change a person so much?

"How do you feel?"

I started at the sound of Opie's voice, then glanced at the clock. It was after ten. "Aren't you late for work?"

"I called in. I figured you would need help to get your car home. Ruby can drive us back to the park." He hesitated. "If you're sure you're up to it, that is."

Shoot, yes. I was up to getting my car, solving Val's death, and maybe even conquering the whole global warming thing while I was at it. Right now, I felt like I could fix all the entire world's problems.

Once I got rid of this nagging headache. Opie brought me a couple of aspirin and a glass of water.

"I know I sound like a broken record, but I still wish you'd agree to be checked out. You could have a concussion from hitting that rock."

"Believe me, I'm fine." I fingered the knot again. It was definitely smaller. "Once the headache goes away, I'll be perfect."

Opie's mouth opened, but nothing came out. He shook his head and turned to the carrier. "I think your cat is waking up."

"Destiny."

He smiled at me. "It's destiny that your cat is waking up? I'd like to think so."

"No, that's his name. Destiny." I glanced under the blanket covering me to make sure I was still dressed—I was—and then threw the covers off and sat up on the edge of the bed. It made my head throb more, but it was good to be mobile again.

After taking care of my most pressing need, I stopped by the carrier to check on Destiny. "You think we should let him out for a little while before we go?"

The alarmed look on Opie's face was almost comically out of proportion to the situation. "He can't stay here! What if he started screeching or something? The whole building would hear him. I happen to enjoy living here, you know."

"Well, we're going to have to work something out with Ruby, then, because I don't think she's quite ready to go home yet."

"Actually, I'll be coming home this afternoon. But I was thinking, since we are all going to get the car, maybe Opie and you could meet me at the rental place and then we could all ride together from there."

Opie looked conflicted. "Then who would drive Amie's car back? I can't drive both cars, and I know her. If it's just the two of you, she'll talk you into letting her drive." He stared into my eyes. "I really don't think that's such a great idea for a day or two, anyway. If you refuse to get checked out, fine, but I'm going with the assumption that you have a concussion. People with concussions shouldn't be driving."

I blew out a big breath. "If it will make things work out, I'll let Ruby drive my car home. And we can drop off the cat at the farmhouse on our way. That should give her time at the rentals to finish up any paperwork before we get there."

I was kind of affronted when he looked to Ruby. "Do you promise not to let her drive?"

She nodded.

Oh sure, he'd believe her. I turned my back to them, grabbed my cat, and walked out. It would have made a much more dramatic exit if I hadn't hesitated by the door. Opie was following so closely behind me that he almost ran into me. Instead, he bumped into the carrier which brought a low growl out of Destiny.

"How do we hide him on the way out? It's not dark now." I really didn't want to cause Opie any major trouble, even if I was a bit ticked off at him right now.

Snapping his fingers, he ran back into his bedroom and returned with an oversized rain poncho. "People might wonder why you're wearing a poncho, but at least it should hide the carrier if you keep it close to your body."

We made it to the car unaccosted by nosy neighbors. Most of them were most likely at work or school anyway. Opie opened the back door for me, and I settled the carrier onto the seat.

"Don't worry, little guy, you'll be home soon."

But once we got to the empty farmhouse—Opal had already left for her shop—I was torn between whether or not to let him roam in the apartment while I was gone. Part of me wanted to give him the space to stretch his legs, but the other part of me really wanted to be there when he first got the full open range. I wasn't used to how cats behaved, and I didn't want to take any chances while we went through the getting to know each other stage of things.

In the end, I made sure his sandbox was okay and put a small bowl of water and a little tuna in with him. That would have to do him until we got back. I'd make sure to give him at least some time out before bed tonight.

Once in the car, with nothing better for my mind to occupy itself with, my thoughts turned once again to Val's death. Something about my visit with Misty was bothering me, but it took a minute for me to put my finger on it. She'd started to imply that maybe her death was because of something she'd done on the council and then backtracked big time.

That was worth checking into. The only bad thing with that angle was that, in a way, it too implicated Opal. After all, Opal was her only opponent in the upcoming elections. Not that Opal would kill for that. Taking her donut, maybe, but a seat on the town council? Never.

I decided a little conversation was in order.

"You know, Opie, when I was talking with Misty Rhodes yesterday something interesting happened."

The car swerved as his eyes flashed from the road to me. And he says I'm a bad driver. Generally, I can keep my eyes on the road, and my car going in a straight line. Unless there's a squirrel. Or a bunny rabbit.

"You do know that you aren't a licensed private investigator yet, right? So, why were you talking to Misty?"

"Last time I heard, you don't have to be licensed just to talk to someone. And besides, the license only matters if you are working for money. This is family—no money involved at all."

He groaned. "I still wish you'd leave this to us. We'll get to the bottom of it, I promise you. Give us some time."

My arms crossed in front of me. "And if you happen to think you find Opal at the bottom? No, thank you. You do your job, and I'll do mine. In case you are wondering, my job is looking out for my family."

After a short pause, he gave up. "All right, tell me. You know you want to."

I thought about playing hard to get. He deserved it for giving me a hard time. But the truth was, I could use his help. Of the two of us, he definitely had more experience in interviewing suspects. I was thinking I could learn something by watching him. And today was the perfect day for that as he was officially off duty.

"Well, Misty suggested that if Val's death was unnatural, the motive might be something to do with her position on the council. But the weird thing is that once she said it, she immediately discounted it and threw Opal under the bus. I'm thinking there's something there that she knows about and is hiding."

"It does kind of sound like it." There was a pause as one hand left the wheel and ran itself through his hair, leaving it in its more natural slightly disheveled shape.

"So, do you want to go back to talk to her? My afternoon is clear once I get my car."

"You think having me there will suddenly open her up and she'll spill everything. Humph, that sure hasn't been my experience up to now. There is another way though. We just check out what she's been working on in the council for the past few months." He paused. "That's actually a good idea."

I sat a little taller. Look at that, not even licensed, and I'd already given the cops a good idea to check out. I was so going to make a good detective. Sherlock Ravenswind, that's me.

"Where do we go for something like that?"

He grinned at me. "You would go to the newspaper archives. I happen to have access to a walking and talking version of that." He pushed a button on his dash and said, "Call Dad." Seconds later, Sheriff Taylor answered.

"Hey, Trevor. How's Amie?"

"She seems to be fine, but I want to keep my eye on her for a little longer to be sure. We're on the way to pick up her car now."

"Then I take it there's something you needed from me?"

"Actually, there is. Amie brought up a good point that maybe Val was up to something, or had done something, on the council that had upset someone. Can you think of anything like that?"

Laughter came through the speakers. "Val Kimble? Up to something someone didn't like? Where do I start?" There was a pause. "But now you mention it, we might want to have a talk with Calvin Brenton. She pretty much nixed a high powered real estate deal he had going by refusing to change the zoning for the property. I seem to remember he fought it hard. Must have meant a lot to him. Financially, if nothing else."

"I might drop by and have a chat with him this afternoon, then. Just kind of feel him out."

There was a moment of silence. "If you take Amie, make sure he knows it's strictly an unofficial visit. And Amie?"

Startled for him to have addressed me, I turned to the dashboard. Where does one look when the voice is coming from speakers? "Yes, sir?"

"Be a mouse. Let Trevor do his job and keep your mouth shut, okay? If you can't do that, then you need to let him do this on his own, got it?"

I swallowed. "Got it, sir."

"Good. Be safe and call me if you get anything."

Opie hit the button to disconnect the call. So that was how men did it. Women, at least the ones in my family, said goodbye at least two and sometimes three times before ending a call.

Chapter 11

Luckily, my car was right where we'd left it, in the parking lot of the small park. The park was a much busier place now, with small children playing on the equipment, and parents laying out blankets full of food to try to entice them over for lunch. Not that it worked, but I gave them kudos for trying.

Ruby's mouth fell open when she saw my car. What? I'd told her the make and model, and she'd even seen it last night. Of course, it had been pretty dark then.

"What happened to your car?" She walked all the way around it, and it didn't take long for the bubbling laughter to make its way out. "You actually drive this? It's an affront to all women."

"So I've been told. And actually, it looks like you'll be driving her today." That'll teach her to make fun of my new baby.

She looked stricken and her pleading eyes turned to Opie. "Please don't make me drive that. What if someone sees me?"

He grinned. "A promise is a promise." But he popped open his trunk and handed her a hat and a scarf. "You can wear these if you want to go undercover. I do."

It kind of surprised me when she took them and put them on. She was really serious? Come on, it was just transportation, right?

The drive back was a silent one with Ruby sulking behind the wheel and ducking every time a car passed us. Once at the farmhouse, she pulled around back, got out, and ran up the stairs.

Opie pulled up beside the car and rolled down his window. "You ready to roll again?"

I glanced up at the balcony entrance and hesitated. "Can you give me just a minute?"

He nodded, and I ran up the steps to check on Destiny. I could have saved myself the stair workout. He was quietly curled up in the corner of the carrier, fast asleep. I jumped when Ruby touched my shoulder.

"Don't be too worried about him sleeping so much. He has a lot to work out of his system. Drugs and magic." She took a deep breath. "You have a lot to learn coming into this so late, but magic really drains you. And if you pull it through your familiar, it drains them too."

Good to know. She was right; I did have a lot to learn. "I didn't hurt him, did I?"

Her answer wasn't as immediate as I would have liked it to be. "I don't think so. I mean he looks well enough, just tired. And besides, if I remember correctly, he slept through the whole thing."

That did make me feel a bit better. I checked his food and water, gave Ruby a quick hug and a peck on the cheek, and ran back down to Opie. Part of me expected him to not be there, but he was.

"Destiny okay?"

"Yup. Sleeping off the last of last night's activity."

He acted like he was going to say something, but if he was, he changed his mind.

It was a short drive into town and Calvin's office. I don't know about Opie, but I was spending it imagining breaking the case wide open on only my second interview. At least until Opie burst my bubble once he'd parked.

"Remember, you agreed to let me do the talking. I believe your exact words to my father were 'yes, sir'."

Crap on toast. Wheat toast, my least favorite.

When we walked in, there was a beeping noise. Most likely it was set up to alert Calvin that he had visitors. His office certainly wasn't on the busy side. In fact, it was empty.

A couple of minutes later, Calvin came rushing in through a side door, straightening his tie. He glanced at us with a smile. As Opie wasn't dressed in his normal uniform, he even kept the smile.

"What can I help you fine folks with today? Looking for a nice little house? It's about time the two of you finally got together."

I shot Opie a covert glance and was surprised to see his cheeks turning red. Going to his rescue might have been an option, but I'd promised to keep my mouth shut. So I did.

"Actually, I wanted to check on the investment deal you had going and see if it was still open for investors."

That was enough for the smile to vanish. Calvin made a face. "Oh, I'd be happy enough to take your money. But I don't think that hotel will ever happen. Sorry." His gaze turned to some papers on his desk, dismissing us.

Opie didn't give up.

"What happened? I thought it was a great idea."

Calvin sighed. "It is a great idea. But without the zoning change, the biggest investor backed out of the deal. You can't put up a hotel in a residential neighborhood without the proper regulations being modified by the town council."

"I take it they didn't agree to the modifications?"

"I had two of the three in my pocket so to speak, but Valerie Kimble was a regular thorn in my side. 'I don't want my hometown turned into nothing more than a tourist attraction'. Shoot, a hotel would be great for this place. Bring in business and help the town grow. Not that I could convince her of that."

"But now that Valerie's no longer a member of the council, do you think they might approve the zoning change?"

Calvin gave a bitter laugh. "You'd like to think so, but no. Opal Ravenswind is the likely replacement for her seat on the council and if there was one single thing the two of them agreed on, it was that the town of Wind's Crossing was better off without a hotel."

I hated to admit it, but he was probably right about that. Which took away any motivation he might have had to do away with Valerie.

"Wait a minute." Calvin looked at me, then back to Opie. "That's what this visit is really about, isn't it? Misty said you guys might come here ask—," he broke off mid-sentence.

I opened my mouth but closed it when Opie's elbow made contact with my ribs. Ouch.

"So, you must know Misty pretty well, then?" Opie asked, innocence pouring out of him.

Calvin swallowed and threw a nervous glance at the side door. "No, not really. We just bump into each other now and then around town."

It disappointed me that Opie let it drop there, but he did.

"Well, thank you for your time." Opie grinned at him. "Hope we didn't interrupt anything important."

"Not at all, not at all." He walked us to the door and opened it for us, ushering us past him and out onto the sidewalk. "But just for the record, if Val's death turns out to be murder, I think it most likely stems from her being a witch." When I made a quick move toward him, he held up one hand. "I'm not implying Opal Ravenswind had anything to do with it."

He gave the side door another furtive glance before leaning in and lowering his voice. "There are a lot of religious fanatics in the town, and some of them really hate witches."

Then he shut the door in our faces and flipped the open sign to closed for lunch. Huh, he probably should have done that before going into that side room to begin with.

I contained myself until we got into the car. Barely, but I did it.

"Misty Rhodes and Calvin Brenton are having an affair, aren't they?"

"I'd say there was an inordinately high probability that is the case."

I just looked at him. "You know you could be normal for once and just say yes."

He grinned at me. "I could. But then how would you grow your vocabulary?"

Opie could be so maddening sometimes. With most people, he was the nice, polite young son of the sheriff. Put him with me, and there was an inordinately high probability that he was going to turn into a horse's patootie at some point.

Pluck a duck! Had I really just used his new vocabulary phrase in a sentence? I gave him an extra glare and then realized that Opie still hadn't started the car.

Not that I would give him the satisfaction of asking why we weren't leaving. My stubbornness turned out to be in my favor a minute later when Misty's blue Toyota came barreling out of the alley.

I waited until it had disappeared around a corner before turning to Opie. "She was in that back room the whole dang time, wasn't she?"

"I'd say there was an inordinately high—oof!"

The 'oof' came when I punched him in the arm. Opie had told me many times that my playful punches are a lot more painful than playful. This one wasn't intended as play.

"Anybody ever tell you that you hit like a guy?"

"I'll take that as a compliment." Then I reached back and fastened my seat belt. "Where to next? Should we try to corner Misty?"

He laughed. "I'm glad one of us got a good night's sleep. But to answer your question, I'm taking you home to your new cat and then I'm going home to take a nap on my nice soft bed."

Oh sure, ratchet up the guilt, why don't you? It wasn't like I'd asked him to hover over me all night.

"You do know that bed was plenty big enough for the two of us, right?"

He blushed and then pulled out into traffic without really looking first. A guy on a scooter laid on his horn and flipped us off. I looked out the window and smiled.

Yeah, like I was the one that shouldn't be driving.

Chapter 12

Opie dropped me off, and I climbed the outside stairs to my shared balcony. Ruby wasn't about, but that didn't surprise me. Chances were good she'd rescued Yorkie Doodle from downstairs and was taking him for an extra-long walk. Opal didn't mind pet sitting, but her idea of giving the dog exercise was letting him out into the backyard. That wasn't what the little guy was used to.

I plopped down on my rocking chair. It was nice to have the house to myself. Opal off at work, Ruby out with YD, all was quiet. Perfect for thinking. I had a lot of that to do.

As I rocked back and forth, I let my mind wander to the conversation with Calvin and its conclusion. He and Misty were most definitely having an affair. In my book, that brought Misty in as a suspect too. Calvin was married to a pretty powerful woman. She was an attorney in the next town over—far too big of a name for our little legal needs to fill. Everyone in town always said that he stayed with her for the money. It wasn't like she spent much time in Wind's Crossing, or with her husband for that matter.

He was arm candy for events and dinners with high-powered corporate clients. Nothing more, it seemed. I could kind of understand him looking for a little affection on the side. A man's got to get it from someone, I guess. At least that's what everyone seems to say.

That could also explain why Misty clamped her mouth shut so tight after mentioning the fact that it might have had something to do with council business. What if she hadn't thought things through like Calvin had and had decided to make things easier for her man? The hotel deal would have made him a pile of money. Money that could have made a new start for the two of them, if he'd chosen to make a break for it.

Of course, as I was thinking about it, I had to also consider the possibility that Calvin had thrown out. The religious fanatics like Mrs. Naomi Hill. I knew for a fact she hated us with a passion. But my thoughts didn't linger too long with her or her ilk. Part of being religious was accepting the entire doctrine. And there was that whole Thou Shalt Not Kill commandment too.

I just couldn't see her risking eternal damnation just to take out a single witch for dancing naked around a bonfire and believing there was a Goddess that went along with the God. I'd been wrong before, and I was sure I'd be wrong again, but it didn't feel right to me.

At this moment, Misty Rhodes was looking like prime suspect number one.

I heard a yowl of frustration and immediately felt guilty. Here I'd been sitting rocking away and Destiny was inside all caged up. I'd promised him some time out. Time to make good on that. Misty would wait.

When I opened the door into the sitting room, I saw two paws sticking out through the bars of the kennel door. They were working furiously trying to open the latch mechanism. Even as I watched, he almost made it. After the failure, he let out another yowl.

Wow. Opie had been right. If he had done that back at his apartment, the whole place would have heard him. Cats can be loud when they want to express their displeasure. Good to know.

I bent down to look at him and made sure he saw me. "Hey, Destiny. I'm home now, and I'm going to let you out for a while, okay?" But before I did, I took a little stroll around the apartment looking for places he might be able to get into that I couldn't get him out of. In the end, I shut off my bedroom and the bathroom and let him out. That gave him access to two of my three rooms. The bedroom he would have to earn by behaving.

When I opened the door, he shot out like lightning, moving so fast he was almost a blur. I managed to track him, but he didn't make it easy. Destiny was fast. Like, really fast.

Once he finally stopped moving, he was on the back of the couch, looking around him with a frantic expression on his face. No doubt wondering exactly where he was and how he came to be here. After all, he'd slept through the move, and who knows what those sleepy time drugs did to him, or how long they affected one after they started to wear off.

"It's okay, fella." I was trying for soothing, but to be truthful, his utter panic was almost catching. "This is your new home. I got you out of there before they could cut off your favorite parts. That's something, right?"

His little green eyes locked onto mine and his head tilted slowly. I could see the recognition growing in them. He remembered me. That was a start.

"I took a big risk getting you, just so you know. If I'd been caught, I could have gone to jail. So you owe me." There, I'd said it. I was a firm believer in laying out the groundwork for a new relationship right up front. Then I softened and made a face. "By the time I got there, they had you all drugged up. That's why you slept so long."

Well, that and the fact I had pulled a massive amount of magic through him somehow. Something I was bound to do again at some point soon. Hopefully, I'd have learned to control it by then.

He was still staring intently at me. It looked like he was trying to ask me something. Oh yeah, the whole where am I thing. I guess telling someone they're in their new home really doesn't answer a lot.

"This is an old farmhouse. I share it with my family." I motioned around me. "But this space is just for the two of us. My cousin, Ruby, lives just across the hall." I chewed my lip. "She has a dog, but nothing for you to worry about. You could easily take him if it came to it. My aunt lives downstairs and whenever my mom's home, she does too. Each on separate sides of the house like Ruby and me."

He was still staring. What else could he want to know?

"Once we get to know each other and establish some ground rules of behavior, you'll have a lot more freedom, I promise. But for now, this is your domain."

Time to let him explore a bit without me yammering on at him. I went into the kitchen to deal with the sink full of dishes that had been waiting for me for a day or two. I should have done them while he was still sleeping. I didn't want him to think I was a slob or something. But then there weren't all that many.

I was just putting them away, when Destiny came walking in, surveying his surroundings. He walked over to the first shut door and pushed his nose against it, then looked at me.

"That's the bathroom. Where we humans go to pee and poop. You'll have your litter box." Which reminded me. It was still in my trunk along with the bag of litter I'd picked up yesterday before my illegal mission. I made sure we had eye contact before I continued. "I have a proper box for you, but until I get it set up, you use the little one in the kennel. Got it?"

I could have sworn he thought about it before his head inclined just a tad. I'd take that as a yes.

He took a nonchalant stroll over to the last closed door as I wiped off the counter and sink and hung up my dishcloth. There, all sparkly clean. See, no slobs here. Well, as long as he didn't make it into the bathroom before I had a few minutes in there. Last time I noticed, the hamper was overflowing. Doing a few loads of laundry was in my near future. Either that or a shopping spree for more clothes. That sounded a lot more fun.

When he put a paw up on the door, I smiled at him. "That's my bedroom and the last room in our space. You have to earn your right to go in there, okay? Let's start with these two rooms and go from there."

That seemed to make him happy enough, at least to his living space. Then he spied the refrigerator. His eyes got a glint to them.

I laughed. "Tired of tuna? Would you like some milk?" I didn't wait for an answer. Taking a small bowl from the cupboard, I filled the bottom of it with fresh milk and sat it on the floor.

Destiny looked at it and then back to the refrigerator.

"Start with the milk, and in a minute, I'll see what else I can scrounge up that's palatable for cats. I'll get you some proper cat food next time I'm in town." Duh, feeding him was probably an important thing. How could I remember the litter box and litter and forget the food?

My cell phone rang in the sitting room, and I had to run for it. The Darth Vader theme from Star Wars was the alert that my aunt was calling. I was really hoping it wasn't bad news.

"Hey, Opal, is everything okay?"

A dry chuckle came through the line. "Well, they haven't arrested me yet, if that's what you're asking." She paused. "I was just calling to see that you made it home okay. It isn't like you to spend the night at Opie's. I'm hoping that means you finally gave the boy a break."

Crapsnackles! I hadn't thought to ask Ruby or Opie what the cover story for last night was. All I knew was that I had to keep Ruby out of it. It would really help right now if I only knew what they'd told her.

When I didn't respond right away, she continued. "Let me guess, you didn't. You really did fall asleep on his sofa watching Ghostbusters, didn't you?"

She sounded disappointed. What on earth had she been expecting to happen? The whole town seemed to think there was something between Opie and me, but I would have thought surely Aunt Opal knew better. We were just friends. Why break a good thing?

"Well, I have seen it a gazillion times, you know." There, the truth. I felt a lot lighter now. That was almost too easy.

"Ah well, a gal can hope. By the way, we're all getting together to make dinner tonight in your mom's kitchen. Ruby called dessert, so you're in charge of peeling the potatoes."

"Maybe we could have stuffing instead?" That was so much easier to make. Stove Top was my best friend.

"Nope, I have my heart set on mashed potatoes. We're just getting ready to leave the shop now. See you in a few minutes."

I was guessing the we she spoke of was her and Ruby. That must have been where the long walk took her and Yorkie Doodle.

If I wanted to gain a little favor in Opal's eyes, I'd go down right now and get started. But I really hated peeling potatoes. We all did. It was the least liked part in the making of the meal. Unfortunately, we all really loved the resulting mashed mounds of goodness.

When I turned, I found two little green eyes staring at me. Okay, that would definitely take some getting used to. I was far too accustomed to living alone. Sharing my living space was going to take some adjustments.

He turned back toward the kitchenette and walked up to the refrigerator. The milk didn't look as though it had been touched. Who knows? Maybe I got a lactose intolerant cat. I already knew he was a bit of a freak of nature, so that wouldn't surprise me.

"Okay, let's see what I have in here." I opened it and looked. Hmm, it was really past time for a grocery run. There were about a half dozen eggs, a couple sausage links, a few tiny mushrooms, and some shredded cheese. In the back, I found an opened package of bologna, but an exploratory whiff said that would be a no go.

Basically, I had all the fixings for an omelet, but I wasn't about to start things off by cooking a full meal for a cat. He needed to learn right off the bat that I wasn't going to cater to his every whim.

I pulled out one of the sausage links, wrapped it in a paper towel and threw it in the microwave. Then I got the little dish out of his kennel and rinsed it off. I sprinkled a small mound of cheese on the dish and when the oven dinged, I crumbled the sausage next to it.

"Careful, it's hot." Hopefully, he'd forgive me for what was about to come next.

He sniffed the offering for a second or two and then dove in. Hey Mikey, he likes it! The potatoes could wait another few minutes. I sat down on the floor next to him and started petting him.

The purring started soon after. The low rumbling sound seemed to startle him, and his head popped up in mid-chew. Poor little guy.

"You must not have had too much to purr about lately if you've forgotten what it sounds like." I scratched the top of his head softly. "That all changes now, Destiny. I'll give you lots to purr about, I swear it. You'll be happy here."

His eyes seemed a little sad as they gazed back at me, but then his hunger won out and he turned back to the food. It didn't last long. I waited until he'd swallowed the last bite before I scooped him up and headed for the kennel.

When he saw where we were headed, he wasn't happy. Squirming, he tried to make it out of my arms, but I held on tight.

"It's just for a little while. I've been summoned to help fix dinner. I won't be gone long at all. You'll have more time out before bed." I thought for a minute. "Actually, if you're good, I might even let you stay out tonight. But I need peace of mind if I have to spend time with Opal. Sorry."

I shoved him in the kennel and then remembered seeing the little paws at work on the latch. Rummaging through my bounty hunting supplies, I came up with a zip tie and used it to secure the door. No way would he get out now. Not until I cut that tie.

He glared at me, and I shrugged at him. "Again, sorry."

Then I grabbed my phone and ran down the inside stairs. I still had time to get started on the potatoes before Opal and Ruby made it home.

Chapter 13

The dinner went well, all things considered. My part of it was especially tasty, I thought. But Opal's fried chicken and Ruby's cherry dump cake—she always did something super easy like that—were good too. Everything hit the spot.

Opal was shocked to learn that I'd recently gotten a cat. Even more shocked to learn that I could be in the same room with him without sneezing and my airways closing up. She looked rather thoughtful.

"Never thought I'd see the day you had a cat. Have you made him your familiar yet or are you getting to know him first? That's never a bad idea, you know. Getting to know them first, I mean. You have a familiar for a very long time. You want to make sure it's one you like. And that they like you. If that isn't the case, forever can be a very long time indeed."

Now she tells me.

"Surely there's some way to break the spell if things don't work out?" There might have been just a touch of desperation in my voice.

Opal smiled grimly. "I'll take that to mean you've already done the spell, and it was a successful one. Let's just say you'd better do everything in your power to make that kitty feel loved and appreciated. It's definitely in both of your best interests."

I swallowed. Funny, I hadn't been all that worried about us getting along until now. Nothing like planting that seed of doubt in my brain.

Not that it had all that much time to grow before the real fun started.

We were finishing up the cleanup, and I was looking forward to a nice quiet evening of watching television and getting to know Destiny better. Then we heard the unmistakable sound of tires on gravel. Two cars pulled up out front. That was unusual in itself.

Known as the go-to source in town for herbal medicine, we were used to having visitors. They didn't, however, usually show up two at a time. Buying potions from witches had seemed to be a very singular activity in the past.

But a look out the window showed that these visitors weren't there for any spells or remedies. Two sheriff's cars were parked out front, and Opie and Sheriff Taylor were climbing out of them.

Opal opened the door before they even had a chance to knock.

"I take it that your presence here means you got the word on Val's death and that it wasn't a good one."

The sheriff nodded. "You're right about that. It was definitely murder."

Opal took a deep breath. "All right then. Do I make my one call from here or the station?"

Ruby started to take a step forward, but I grabbed her arm and shook my head. It wouldn't help Opal to make a scene.

"We aren't here to arrest you." Sheriff Taylor looked past Opal to the two of us and nodded. "Girls." Then he looked back to Opal. "Could we maybe have this conversation inside?"

She looked confused for a second, then stepped back to let them pass. Few people got the chance to remind Opal about guest etiquette. She could have written a book on it. The pressure of the situation had to be weighing heavily on her. After a second's hesitation, she led them into my mom's apartment. It made sense, as that was where we had been when they came.

So far, Opie hadn't said a word, and that had me worried. They might not have come to arrest Opal, but whatever their reason for being there, it wasn't good. I could feel it in my bones.

"Can I get you two something to drink? Or a piece of cherry dump cake?" Opal was trying hard to remedy her earlier hosting error in not inviting them in.

"As good as it smells in here right now, we'll have to decline. We're here on business, not for pleasure, I'm afraid."

But if they weren't here to arrest Opal, then why were they here?

"Please don't tell me that another witch is dead." Opal's voice sounded flat. She sank onto one of Mom's easy chairs and motioned for all of us to sit down too.

That was another reason for using Mom's apartment. Of all of us, she was the only one with the setup for entertaining guests. Plenty of places to sit, and even a corner fireplace and a big screen television.

Opie and his dad shared a glance, and my worry notched up a peg.

"No one else has died yet that we know of." The sheriff's tone didn't suggest that was the good news that it seemed. "But there is something we wanted to share with you in person."

He sat down on the edge of the couch and took a deep breath. Opie sat on the cushion beside him.

"The coroner just released the results of the autopsy a little while ago. Someone poisoned Valerie Kimble." His eyes sought Opal's. "The poison was in the raspberry filling of that donut she took."

I felt light-headed, and Opie handed me a paper bag. He knew my tendency to hyperventilate, and he'd come prepared. Eagle Scouts are like that.

"Then it wasn't Val they were after." Opal sounded very matter of fact about it all. If I'd just learned that I'd narrowly escaped death because a pissed off witch had stolen a poisoned donut meant for me, I wouldn't be nearly so calm about it. "So where do we go from here?"

"Well, for starters, whoever did this didn't get the result they wanted the first time. From everything I've encountered in my career in law enforcement that means they'll likely try again."

Opie leaned in towards my aunt. "Do you have any idea who might want to hurt you?"

"You mean kill me, don't you?"

He flinched but nodded. Opie should know Opal well enough by now to know that she didn't mince words. She was a straight shooter, even in times like this. Maybe especially in times like this.

She thought for a minute. "The one with the biggest motive is dead." Opal looked up at the sheriff. "You already know that me and Valerie didn't see eye to eye on a lot of things."

"Your craft being one of them." The sheriff said it as a fact, not a question. He was right.

"There were other things too, but yes, the craft was the main point of contention between us. She felt that our coven was somehow hogging the Goddess' blessing all for ourselves when we should be sharing them with the likes of herself. I couldn't convince her that some things are simply born into a person. Or not. In my opinion, Misty Rhodes is the only one in the Windsong Coven worth a dadgum. At least when it comes to magic."

"Unfortunately, Valerie Kimble is the one person we can rule out for a multitude of reasons. The main one being she wouldn't have eaten a donut that she herself had poisoned."

Opal looked around the room slowly, as if something there might jog her memory and come up with another, still living, suspect. In the end, she just shook her head. "I can't think of anyone else with a reason to want me dead."

"How about Naomi Hill?" Opie asked quietly. "Everyone in town knows she is jealous of you. She'd never have gotten George Hill to begin with if you hadn't turned him down cold."

"But she got him in the end, didn't she?" Opal gave a dry laugh. "Oh, yes, I'm well aware that he still likes to spy on our coven meetings. I can't very well stop him, now can I? So I do the next best thing. I ignore him, and any other men that might watch too. As I've never once encouraged him, I can't see her being willing to hang up her religious principles just to wipe me off the planet."

I swallowed. I'd seen the inside of Naomi's home once, when I'd been after Tommy for bond jumping. I still shivered just remembering that sign quoting the bible over her fireplace. Thou shalt not suffer a witch to live. Perhaps Opie had something there. I might have discounted her a little too quickly.

"Has anything odd happened lately that you can remember?" Sheriff Taylor asked softly. "Anyone unusual or strange come to you for an item? Any odd visitors at the shop?"

"You mean the back room at the shop, don't you? I think the time for pussyfooting around this has passed, Orville. You want to know if a fellow witch could be behind this?"

He nodded. "I do. If I'm right, those donuts were just sitting out pretty much in the open at your coven meeting. Any of the witches there could have shot the poison into the filling of your donut."

She looked thoughtful. "You are right there. So they would definitely have had the opportunity." She sighed. "Now if we can match that up with someone with motive, we'd have it made." Opal glanced over at Opie. "But that seems to knock out Naomi Hill as a suspect. I don't know when she would have had the opportunity to poison that donut."

Dang. She had a point. And I was really warming to her being the one behind all this too. But then I thought of Tommy. Maybe her not being the guilty party wasn't such a bad thing.

What with the hacking charges, probation, and secret government work, he had enough on his plate without adding a murderous mother to it.

"Am I wrong to think there's a reason the two of you each brought your own car?" Opal was on a roll. I hadn't even considered that. Now she mentioned it though, it was odd.

"I was kind of hoping I could camp out here of a night and help keep an eye out for you for a few days," Opie said, with a quick glance at me. "I'd hate to have something happen to my favorite witches."

Opal grunted. "Well, you can suit yourself." She glanced around, then over to me. "I don't think Sapphire would mind if he stayed here for a few days, do you?"

Now why didn't I think of that? Here I'd been trying to come up with a reason not to have him camp out on my sofa when right below lay the perfect solution. An entire, empty apartment.

"I'm sure she'd be okay with that." Was it just me or did Opie look a little relieved too? Somehow that made me feel better, even though I probably should have taken it as an insult. I was trying hard to stay on the positive side of things. This way, he could help keep watch, and we could both keep our privacy. Win-win.

"Well, now that that's settled," the sheriff said, standing up. "I'd better head home and let my dog out. He's probably wondering where I am about now."

Opal stood and walked him to the door. The two of them had a short conversation too quiet for the rest of us to hear. I was a tad bit surprised when Opal kissed his cheek before he left.

I took my cue from the sheriff. "I'm going to turn in for the night too. Maybe watch some television and snuggle with my new furry best friend. It's time to create a bit of bonding between us."

"Kind of like shutting the barn door after the horse is out, but better late than never." Opal turned to Ruby. "I think I will turn in, too, dear. Unless you wanted to watch a movie or something at my place?"

She looked a little relieved when Ruby shook her head. "I'll take a rain check on that. Right now, I'm going upstairs and climb into the bed I've missed so very much with a good book and my little dog."

I glanced at Opie, feeling a little bad that we were just leaving him here all alone. "Will you be okay down here by yourself?"

He gave me a sad smile. "I'll manage. Let me run out to my car, first, though, to grab my things."

The trip only took a minute, and when he returned, he was carrying not one, but two bags. Just how long did he intend to stay, anyway? When he bent over to set them down, I saw the glint of metal. He might be in plain clothes, but he was wearing his sidearm. More than almost anything else I'd seen or heard, that brought our situation all home to me. We were in danger.

As I walked up the stairs, I found I was very glad that Opie would be sleeping right below me.

Chapter 14

When I cut the tie and opened the kennel door, Destiny still sat inside, glaring at me.

"Look, I really don't need the attitude right now, okay? I've just learned that someone tried to kill my aunt a couple nights ago and now it looks like maybe we're all in danger. So I could really just use a nice, soft, friend right now, okay?"

He looked a bit surprised, but the only thing that mattered to me was that he came out.

"I brought you a little something from dinner to make it up to you." I held out the small baggie of plucked up chicken that I'd saved from the last piece. My aunt had warned me just in time that I shouldn't give a cat anything with chicken bones. I'd planned to give him the whole dang piece. This was safer.

I pulled out his plate and sat the chicken on it, then pulled the water dish from the kennel too. It was time to make a stand. Once the daily necessities were out of the cage, including the makeshift litter box, I put the carrier in the hallway for Ruby to pick up the next time she came out.

Unless I was mistaken, Destiny's eyes gleamed a little as it went out the door. Hopefully, that didn't mean he was planning something nefarious, but from what I knew of him so far, he most likely was. We truly were meant for each other. We could make this work, I just knew it. Opal was only trying to scare me. I might not always do things her way, but I generally came out okay.

I looked him in the eyes. "I'm going out to my car to get the new litter pan and supplies. You will not try to run out on me, or I'll bring in the carrier. Understand?"

He didn't dignify me with an answer. Instead, he turned his back to me, raised his tail to full height and went over to the chicken and started eating. I took that as a yes.

Still, I ran down and back in record time. He was just finishing when I came back in. He sniffed the water dish and then sneezed.

"What, you want wine instead?"

He tilted his head at me. Oh, what the heck. I was going to open that bottle in the fridge, anyway.

I pulled it out. It was a sweet dessert wine—my favorite kind. Perfect for the occasion. I popped the cork with a little show of force and poured a nice tall glass for myself. Then I got out a saucer and poured an experimental little dab out for him.

He drank it. Every last drop. Then he looked up at me for more. I shrugged and poured him another saucer full.

"Okay, but don't blame me if you wake up in the morning with a hangover." Who knew how much wine a cat could hold without getting full on drunk? More importantly, were cats mean drunks or mellow ones? I probably should have thought of that before I'd given Destiny an alcoholic beverage. Now, I'd just have to hope for the best.

Kind of like I had to do with the whole getting to know an animal before making him your lifelong companion kind of thing. I was a true work in progress.

I sat on the floor shuffling through my rather extensive movie selection, trying to find one to watch while I dozed off. That was my usual nightly routine. Climb into bed, pop a movie into the player hooked up to my bedroom television and watch until I couldn't keep my eyes open any longer. Opie had helped me rig it to automatically turn off once the movie finished playing.

To me, sometimes technology is every bit as mysterious as magic. And just as foreign to me, too.

Destiny watched me for a minute and then came ambling over to me to check out the selection. There was a definite list to his walk. Note to self: cut him off at two saucers of wine. A little drunken swagger was fine. Throwing up on my shoes, on anywhere else in my apartment, wasn't.

He tilted his head back and forth as he walked among the discs spread out over the floor. I pulled three toward me and steered him toward them.

"These are the three final contestants for the evening's viewing hour." He looked up at me, then down at my final choices. Then he sneezed and walked over to one I'd already discounted as far too violent for a pre-bed showing. He put his paw on my copy of Taken and looked at me.

I shook my head. "No way. As much as I love Liam Neeson, I'm not risking those kinds of dreams tonight. I want something light and funny for the evening." I glanced back down to my choices. "How about Clue? It's great for laughs, and you gotta love Tim Curry, right?"

He sneezed again. Okay, so my cat has no taste when it comes to comedy. Tim Curry is the bomb in that movie, and the rest of the cast is pretty dang awesome too.

The next time, he rested his paw on an old monster flick. One of the cheesy vampire ones that seem to find their way into my collection.

"Sorry, but that's strike two. I said I wanted funny. I'll give you one chance to pick out a comedy, any comedy, or I'm going with Clue."

His head wiggled back and forth, as if he were trying to decide, then finally his paw reached out and tapped another case with a look of pure satisfaction. I glanced down and groaned. No doubt he and Opie were destined to become the very best of friends.

"All right. Just this one time. But tomorrow night I get to choose, and it'll be Clue."

Then came the important decision-making time. Did I let him into my bedroom, or not? I could see pluses and minuses from both angles. But as I was trying to go all out in forming a lasting relationship here, I decided open doors might be the best. Besides, no way was I going to suffer through Ghostbusters again alone.

He acted affronted when I scooped him up in my arms, but when his eyes landed on my boobs, he calmed. And leered. I swear I have the weirdest feline in the entire world. That, or at the very least the most expressive. It was enough to kind of creep me out.

I sat him down on the bedroom floor and grabbed my pajamas. I'd be changing in the bathroom tonight.

When I came out after my nightly process, he was already camped out on my bed. That would have been fine, but he was on my side. Boundaries had to be established right from the start. Sleeping on the bed was allowed, but the right side was mine. He wasn't happy about it, but as he was a cat, and therefore easy to move, he didn't really have a choice.

I popped the disc into the player, moved him to the left side, and settled in. When he saw that his glares were doing no good, and I wasn't trading spots, Destiny eventually got the hint about the status quo and settled in too.

When the movie started, his eyes were glued to the set. I wondered if other cats liked to watch television too, or if it was just another of Destiny's quirks. Either way, I'd take it. Watching movies together could be a good bonding experience.

***

I remembered watching them find the old firehouse and move in, but then it was lights out for me. Until I heard the noises coming from the other rooms. It finally hit my sleepy brain that I didn't live alone anymore, and a quick glance confirmed that the little furry body was no longer lying beside me.

Rolling over, I shut my eyes to go back to sleep. Then I heard the unmistakable sound of my computer turning on. What the heck?

Throwing the covers off, I reached by the bed and grabbed my baseball bat. Yes, I lived in a house full of powerful witches, but sometimes the oldies were just goodies. I could have grabbed my taser, but it was in the sitting room closet in my bounty hunter backpack. That would change after tonight.

I crept quietly out of my bedroom. My computer was sitting on my little table for two. I was positive it hadn't been there when I laid down.

I was also positive that there hadn't been a naked man going through my refrigerator when I laid down either. But there was one there now.

Scratch that. There was a gorgeous naked man going through my refrigerator. Well, I was assuming he was naked. His hair was wet, and he had one of my pink bath towels wrapped around his waist. Moisture still gleamed on his muscular arms and legs.

What kind of burglar or would be murderer uses their victim's shower and computer?

As he hadn't yet seen me, I thought about going through and trying to retrieve my taser, but that was too risky a move. Didn't the movies teach me anything? You never leave an enemy behind you.

Not knowing exactly how to handle the situation, I was still standing there dumbfounded when he finally took his head out of the refrigerator and turned around. He was holding the makings of an omelet. Basically, the entire contents of my fridge.

He almost dropped them when he saw me standing there. Well, that and the fact that I hefted my bat and took a step toward him.

The items went on the counter, and he held up both hands. The sudden movement must have been just enough to loosen the knot on the towel because it fell to the floor.

Now that I got a full frontal view of the man, I had to confirm my earlier assessment. The guy was absolutely stunning. An Adonis. And someone I had never seen before in my life. I'd have remembered him, trust me.

"Don't do anything you're going to regret." His voice was cultured and deep. What they call a bedroom voice. "I'm going to bend down and retrieve my towel. Don't freak out and take a swing at me."

"Pretty sure you'd be the one to regret that." But I took a step back, got my bat into a position to swing, and nodded at the towel. I wanted answers, and they wouldn't come if I bashed him unconscious.

He bent quickly and retied it around his waist. The thing I noticed was that he didn't seem overly embarrassed about being caught with his pants—or rather towel—down. Obviously, he was very comfortable showing off his body.

"Is that the new thing now? Burglars taking showers and using their victim's computers?" I mean, why didn't he just take the darn thing? He could have used it when he got back to his own place. Could have showered there too.

He took a long breath and just stared at me. "Look, we need to talk. I'm not a burglar. I'm…"

Whatever he was going to say never made it out of his mouth because just at that moment, we both heard heavy footsteps pounding up the staircase. My head swung toward my bedroom door looking for the latest menace before I remembered Opie was downstairs.

I realized my mistake as Opie came bursting through into my kitchenette. I'd given the enemy my back. Any second now there would be a knife at my throat, and I'd be a hostage.

Only it never happened. When I turned back to the gorgeous naked man, trying to think how on earth I would explain him to Opie, he wasn't there. Instead, Destiny sat there in the middle of an oversized pink bath sheet. Once again, his eyes were pleading. As if they were begging me not to tell.

That's when everything went dark.

Chapter 15

I kept my eyes closed even after I came to, listening to the voices that surrounded me. Ruby, Opie, and Opal. Once again, Opie was all for calling in the medical paramedics, but my aunt wasn't having any of it.

"She's fine." Then she paused. "Although in all her life, I've never known her to faint before. I'd have said it wasn't in her. You'd best tell me exactly what happened." Another slight pause. "And you can open your eyes any time now, girl. I know you're back with us."

I did. Opie must have carried me into the sitting room because I found myself on the sofa. The first thing I did was search the room for Destiny. It didn't take long to find him. He was lying on the back of the sofa staring at me with those pleading eyes of his.

"At the risk of repeating myself, I'm still waiting to hear what happened up here." Opal's eyes bore into mine. "You aren't the kind of girl to faint on the drop of a dime. You're sterner stuff than that."

How do you tell someone that you're pretty sure your cat is really a man? A gorgeous, gloriously handsome, naked man. Call me slow, but that's when what I'd done finally hit me. If Destiny was actually a human man, then I'd just made another human my familiar.

My breath started coming faster, and Opie handed me a bag. I nodded my thanks to him. Really, I needed to start carrying them myself. Or learn how to control myself better. One or the other for sure.

As I tried to slow my breathing down by concentrating on filling and emptying the paper bag, my eyes landed on Opie's belly button. His bare belly button. Then they traveled over chiseled abs and up to his bare muscular chest. Who knew Opie Taylor had a six-pack?

Something small in my heart shifted, but I pushed the sensation to one side. I had enough crises already. I really didn't think I could handle another right now. Breathe in, breathe out. That was important.

Opie took over. "I have no idea why she fainted, but at least I can give you my side of the story. I was downstairs on the couch and I heard her start watching Ghostbusters. Awesome choice, but just for the record, I never want to hear complaints about it again. I figured she dropped off sometime before it was over, and it shut itself off at the end. I woke up when I heard footsteps and then the shower running. I thought it was odd, but nothing to worry about. Then I heard her walk toward the kitchen."

He paused, looking at me. I was avoiding his eyes, and he knew it.

"That's when it really got odd, though, because I heard footsteps coming out of her bedroom into the kitchen area. Where she already was, or so I thought. Then I could have sworn I heard a man's voice. She wasn't screaming, so I took the time to throw on my sweats and I ran up here. Just after I got here, she looked over at her cat and just went down." He hesitated. "At least she didn't hit her head or anything when she went down. I made it to her in time."

"Was there anyone else up here?" Opal asked, her eyes on me.

Opie shook his head. "Just her and the cat, and I'm pretty sure I would have heard them leave too."

Opal looked thoughtful but waited until my breathing was pretty much normal. She always knew. "Whenever you're ready, I'm sure we're all on pins and needles."

There were only two ways to explain what happened. The truth, which might make me sound more than a little crazy, or a slight fabrication that would just make me seem extremely stupid. For Destiny's sake, and yes, my own, too, I chose the stupid one.

I tried out a hollow laugh. "I fell asleep watching the movie with Destiny, and I guess I must have had a bad dream or something because I woke up. Then I remembered that the shirt I really wanted to wear today was wrinkled and I wouldn't have time to wash and dry it. So I got up and hung it in the bathroom and let the hot water run to build up steam."

I shrugged. "Then I went into the kitchen and decided to make an omelet. Opie startled me running up the steps like that and then when I turned back to the kitchen Destiny ran out and… I don't know, really. Maybe I thought he was a rat or something? For a minute I think I forgot I had a cat now. I might not have been as fully awake as I thought I was."

As I've said before, Opal has always been able to tell when I was lying. Luckily, this time if she knew, she didn't press it. More than likely she thought I'd had a male visitor and come close to getting caught. Don't get me wrong, I could have guys spend the night whenever I wanted. I just had never wanted to yet.

"And the extra footsteps and man's voice I heard?" Opie, however, would not let it go.

I shook my head and smiled at him. My brain just couldn't come up with a logical explanation. "As you said, there was only me and the cat. I'm not sure what you heard.

Could you have been dreaming?" If you wanted to get super technical, all of that was true. But the disappointed look on Opie's face just about broke my heart. He deserved better than that. So much better.

"Are you okay now?" Opal asked. "Maybe one of us should stay up here with you for the rest of the night."

"No!" Okay, that came out a little too strong. "I mean no, that isn't necessary. You all have work tomorrow. I was just being stupid. Right now I'm just going to scoop up Destiny and go back to sleep." And if there had been a way I could backtrack and remove my permission for Opie to be sleeping directly underneath me, I would have. As it was, I was just going to have to take precautions.

Opal and Opie went back downstairs, but Ruby stayed. When I could tell that they had reached the bottom of the steps, and thus wouldn't hear, I did something I never do. I locked my bedroom door.

When I rejoined Ruby and Destiny in the sitting room, my cat was in her lap purring and rubbing against her. That was so wrong. And Destiny needed to know one thing right up front. I might lie to Opal and Opie, but Ruby was different. We didn't keep secrets from each other.

"So what really happened?" Ruby asked with a knowing smile. "And who was he?"

I took a deep breath. "I do believe he's the one snuggling deep into your lap right now."

Her petting hand stopped in mid-motion. Then she carefully reached down and picked him up and put him on the cushion beside her. "Oh, crap, this is bad."

See why we didn't keep secrets? It was kind of like we shared a brain or something. Give Ruby just one little detail and she was instantly onboard. The others might have thought I was crazy. Ruby? She totally believed me.

"I know, right?" Then I remembered the listening man downstairs. Holding up one finger, I went over and turned on the stereo. Soft classical music came drifting through the room. It should be enough to help cover our conversation, as long as we kept our voices low. After all, I don't think he actually heard the words, just the tone of voice.

The bad thing was that Opie wasn't a stupid man. He'd know the music for what it was. A cover up. I hated hurting him even more, but right now it just couldn't be helped. I'd have to try doubly hard to make it up to him later, once I knew exactly what I'd gotten myself into.

Ruby slowly stood and then came over to me. "If he isn't just a cat, then you know he has to be a witch, right?" Then she hesitated. "Or possibly a shifter, though I've never actually met one."

Dang it. I hadn't really thought about that. If he was a witch, then maybe I really didn't have any magic after all. It was entirely possible that I'd just pulled his magic from him. When I remembered that oak tree, I felt lightheaded again.

"I've got to sit down."

Once we were both settled, Ruby turned to Destiny. "We need to talk. Change."

Very slowly the cat looked from me to her, then shook his head.

I turned to my cousin in consternation. "Okay, well, if he won't change then I guess there's nothing to it. Bring in the carrier and we'll lock him up for the night."

That got a response. He meowed, then sat down and shoved his nose in his crotch. He'd be great at charades.

When I realized his reason for not changing, I laughed. "I don't think he wants you to see him naked." Though for the life of me, I couldn't understand why. He hadn't seemed all that shy in front of me.

"Hmm. Hold that thought." Ruby left and then came back with a pair of cutoff sweatpants and an extra-large T-shirt. She showed them to him and then put them inside the bathroom. "The shorts might be a little tight on you, but the elastic is good."

Destiny hesitated, then went into the bathroom. A second later the door was pushed closed. When it reopened the gorgeous man from before was standing there. All six feet something of him. I heard Ruby's sudden intake of breath.

"I totally get the fainting thing now." She swallowed and then tore her eyes from him to me. "And he was naked?" Her voice squeaked just a bit on that last word.

"As a newborn babe." Then I thought about it. "Well, he had a towel for a while before he lost it."

"Ah yes, that would explain the shower thing."

"Ahem." Destiny must not be used to being ignored.

When I turned to him, I found that Ruby was most definitely correct about one thing. He was for sure a witch. I really didn't think shifters had the ability to float inches off the floor. He mimed walking over to us and settled on the chair beside the couch. I say mimed because even though he went through the motions of walking, his feet never touched the carpet.

"Cool levitation spell," Ruby said. "Don't suppose you'd be willing to share that one?"

He smiled at her. "Let's see how the rest of this evening goes and then we'll talk about it." Then he glanced at the floor. "That man is right below, isn't he? Should one of us do a noise cancellation spell?"

"Go ahead." My cousin was cool as a cucumber. Me? I was totally freaking out again. But then, of the two of us, I was the one who had just made a powerful witch my familiar. Somehow, I was guessing he didn't know that yet. I wasn't looking forward to him finding out either.

A small chant and a couple of complex finger movements later, a thin blue haze settled just above the carpet. "That should do it."

If I didn't know any better, I'd think he was showing off. Not for me, either. No, his eyes were drawn repeatedly to Ruby. He must have a thing for blondes. Fine by me. I didn't need yet another complication thrown into this mess. There was enough on my plate already.

He smiled at Ruby. "So, where do we start?"

She looked over at me. Yeah, she was worried too. It would appear that he was much more powerful than the two of us combined. Possibly even a match for the great and mighty Opal Ravenswind herself. It might not have been such a great idea to do this without her. But then again, if there was a way to reverse the spell, maybe she'd never have to know?

I bet that wouldn't be the case, but one could hope. But first things first, I had to break the news to Destiny. Although real names might be a good place to start things off.

"Well, you could start by telling us who you are and why you were a cat in an animal shelter when I found you."

His eyes reluctantly left Ruby to focus on me. Hello, I'm your witch, buddy, like it or not. Besides, I'm the one who bloody well saved your cute little patootie. A little respect would be nice.

"Now isn't a good time for me to tell you who I am, and as for why I was hiding out as a cat in a shelter, well, needless to say… I was hiding."

"Let me guess," Ruby said smiling. "It has something to do with an old girlfriend, doesn't it?"

He didn't return her smile, but he did nod. "You could definitely say that, yes." His somber tone spoke volumes. There was something very wrong here.

"Hold on just a minute, guys," I said. "I want to get something before we go any further with this conversation."

The man gave a slow smile. "If you're going for your baseball bat, I can promise you I mean you no harm."

Yeah, well, for one it wasn't the bat I was going for, and for two, he might change his mind when he found out what we'd done to him. I got up and retrieved the taser from the closet but shoved it in the waistband of my pajama pants. My oversized T-shirt top hid it from view. I felt a lot better with a little technological magic on my side. A taser blast was every bit as effective as a magic spell, and a whole heck of a lot faster.

I could hear them behind me. He was really laying it on thick with Ruby. Wouldn't Opal be pleased that I'd brought a powerful male witch in as a suitor for her? Think of the power their child would have. Of course, Ruby had to be willing first. Right now, that didn't seem too certain.

Once I was settled back on the couch, I shifted the conversation back to the important thing. Better to pull that Band-Aid off quickly, and I had to get some sleep tonight. Ruby too for that matter. She really did have to work tomorrow. At least my schedule was clear. One of the perks of being self-employed.

"Okay, so just to lay the groundwork, we truly believed you were nothing more than a cat. A regular old stray cat picked up by the shelter. We're clear on that point, right?"

His gaze shifted to me, his eyebrows drawing together. At that point, I think he was starting to get the idea that something bad was about to be revealed.

"Yes," he drawled, drawing that word out far more than its three letters generally allowed. "And if you are waiting for me to thank you, I will. Thank you. It was pretty hairy in there right at the last."

"Especially when they drugged you." Ruby wanted to make the situation absolutely clear. Not a bad idea at all—I was really glad she was here with me. For more than that reason alone too.

"Ah, that explains the massive headache and lethargy I felt this morning."

Well, it could have, at least in part, but I was betting it was the whole me pulling a massive amount of foreign magic out of him. He saw me look at Ruby.

"What are you not telling me?"

Then, to my horror, he started chanting and moving his fingers. Another thin blue haze of magic formed. This time in a narrow line connecting him to me.

I swallowed and met his eyes. My horror was nothing compared to his.

"What in blazes have you done?" He leaped to his feet, his hair billowing out around him as he took a short step toward me.

Two things happened then. One, I drew my taser and took aim. Two, Ruby quickly got between the two of us. Her hair was billowing as well. Male and female witches in a magical standoff. But at least I had my taser.

I thought maybe he should pay more attention to that fact. I had my finger on the trigger when he finally threw a glance my way. Most likely to assess my magical threat. When he saw the taser, his hair fell. It was kind of funny to watch, actually.

"Don't do something you'll regret."

Too late for that, and I really wished he'd stop telling me that.

"Sit down and stop drawing power, and I'll put the taser away. As long as your proverbial finger is on the trigger, so is mine."

He took a deep, shaky breath. "Fair enough." His face was still flushed with anger, but I could understand that.

I was more than a bit angry myself, and in my mind he was the villain here, not me. Posing as a cat and taking an innocent witch unawares—it just wasn't right, that.

It took a minute more standing off against Ruby, but eventually, he sat. I was guessing he paused only to save face. The thought of all those electrical volts running through you should be enough to give even an ultra-powerful witch a reason to get in line. It was one of the reasons it was my weapon of choice.

"I want you to end this binding immediately." He gritted his teeth as he said it.

"Be happy to, if you would only be so kind as to tell me how to do that."

He flinched and then looked to Ruby, who was still standing. His attraction to her didn't seem nearly as plain now. "You helped her do this, didn't you?"

She nodded. "I did. She needed a familiar, and when she found a cat that didn't make her sneeze, I thought it was Goddess driven. Destiny—like she named you."

"Yeah, we'll get to the whole stripper name later. Right now, we have to figure out how to end this."

Right there with you, buddy. But there was something even more important on my mind at this particular moment in time.

"Look, here's where we stand," I said. "You are hiding from something and won't tell us what. You don't have any money or transportation—or even clothes—so it would appear you are stuck here for a while, anyway. That means we have some time to work through this like the rational witches I hope we all are."

I waited until he gave me a grudging nod. "All right then, I propose we think on this tonight while we sleep and come up with a plan on how to resolve this. In the meantime, the more pressing matter is figuring out sleeping arrangements."

There was no way I was sleeping in the same apartment as a witch I'd bound to me. There was only sure-fire way to end a binding that I knew of.

The death of one of the bound.

Chapter 16

Ruby wasn't all that happy about the solution, but she couldn't come up with a better one. In the end, she fetched Yorkie Doodle and allowed Destiny to stay in her apartment. Then she put a very strong and glowing spell on my door leading out to our small, shared landing. If anyone opened that door before Ruby had a chance to deactivate the spell, we'd hear them. As powerful as she made it, the people in town would probably hear it.

Then we went to bed. I've shared a bed with Ruby before many times. Cousins can do that kind of thing. Nothing hinkier than girl talk ever happened either. She wasn't just my cousin; she was my very best friend.

It took me a while to finally doze back off, and when I woke the next morning Ruby was already gone. Thank goodness we wore the same size in clothes as neither of us had thought for her to grab an extra outfit from her apartment for today. She always worked the morning and early afternoon shift at Opal's shop. So until later today, I'd be on my own with Destiny.

Sorry if he had a problem with that name. Until he was willing to give me another, more accurate, name I was sticking to my guns. Maybe it would be an incentive for him to come clean to us.

The knock at my door startled me. Especially as it was on my bedroom door. Then my sleepy brain remembered Opie. Sure enough, he was standing on the other side.

"I wanted to check in on you before I headed to work. I saw Ruby leave and thought you might be awake." He must have noticed the sleep in my eyes and my bed hair. "Sorry if that wasn't the case."

"Actually, I'd just woken up." I stepped back and motioned for him to come in, but he shook his head. "I really have to be going." His eyes searched out mine. "Are you okay?"

Goddess help me, but I could tell he was hurting. "I'm okay, Opie, but I really appreciate you taking such good care of me."

He looked away. "I'll always be here for you, Amie, no matter what. I want you to know that. But if you have someone else—another man—in your life, I would like to know it."

I swallowed and considered how to respond. Opie and I had been friends since before kindergarten. But just friends. After that slight shift inside last night, I really didn't know if that was still the case any longer. Maybe it had never been the case with him. I was just now starting to understand some of the comments Opal and the folks from town had been making about the two of us. I'd been so clueless before.

"I'm not seeing anyone right now, Opie. You have my word on that. Last night was, well, can I just say there was magic involved and leave it at that?" Again, the truth, just not the whole truth. But maybe it would be enough.

A tiny glimmer of hope lit his beautiful green eyes. How had I never noticed his eyes before?

"That works for now. Is it okay if I stay again tonight? I really don't want you ladies here alone until we get this whole thing sorted out."

I know it was selfish of me, but for a minute I wondered how he knew about Destiny being a witch instead of a cat. Then the whole attempted murder thing came rushing back at me. Oh yeah, that thing.

"I think we'd all appreciate that. As far as I'm concerned, you can stay as long as you like." Or until my mom came home, whichever came first.

He hesitated, then bent down and kissed the top of my head. "Stay safe. Magic can be dangerous when you don't know what you're doing."

Yeah, tell me about it. But what I said was. "I'll be super careful." Then I thought about his day job. "You be careful too, okay?"

I walked him down to his car, and we hugged goodbye. Hugs, I could handle. I would have to take this one tiny step at a time. Old habits and feelings die hard with me.

Once his car was out of sight and out onto the road, I turned to go back in. Opal was blocking the stairs. Crap on toast. I hadn't thought to tell Destiny to cast one of those silent carpet spells in Ruby's apartment. Had she heard him?

"I'd like to talk to you if you have a minute." She didn't have her normal go get 'em voice this morning. In fact, if it hadn't been my aunt Opal I was talking to, I'd say maybe she was a little scared.

"Sure." I followed her into her living room.

"Who's the pretty girl?"

I smiled over at Bridget. She was Opal's Macaw and also her familiar. My aunt had set up her perch in front of the picture window for today. Most likely as an early warning system for unwanted visitors.

I felt kind of bad now that my whole family had chosen familiars other than felines to cater to my allergies. And now, here I have a cat. Well, as far as they know I have a cat. Dang, but that was a complicated situation.

"Bridget's the pretty girl." Trust me, I had to say it. Until she got that response, she just kept repeating the phrase. It got annoying fast.

Opal sat on the sofa and motioned for me to sit. I took the chair across from her. "What did you need to talk about, Opal?"

She wouldn't meet my eyes. "I can't help but wonder if you've come across something in those investigation studies of yours that might tell us where we could start looking for clues as to who is behind all this. I don't like the thought of putting my family in danger."

I wet my lips. They felt parched all of a sudden.

"Well, the main things you look for are motive, means, and opportunity from what I read. Like Naomi Hill might have the motive as she hates our living guts, and she might have the means as poison is pretty readily available, but did she have the opportunity? That kind of thing."

Opal chewed on her bottom lip. Now at least I knew where Ruby got that habit from. I'd never seen Opal so unsure of herself to actually do it. She'd always been rock solid around me. This was a whole new side to her. One I really hoped didn't stick around too long. It was freaking me out.

"What if she had someone do the actual deed for her? Her son, a non-witch, was there that night. Could he have doctored that donut for his mother?"

I shook my head. "No way. Tommy isn't a killer. I'd stake my life on it."

She gave me a sad smile. "Well, dear, hopefully your life isn't the one at stake."

Dang. She had a point. Still, Tommy didn't have the heart of a killer. He was a felon, yes, but a harmless one. At least if you took away his computer.

"I'm sorry, but I don't think Tommy had anything to do with it." But it raised an interesting question. Why had he been there? Why the sudden interest in Wicca and witchcraft? Especially considering his mother was so adamantly opposed to it. "Maybe I should have a talk with him. Now that you mention it, I do wonder why he was even there."

"Yes, so do I." She paused. "Do you think you'd be safe to talk to him? I don't want you or Ruby getting hurt in all this."

"I'll be fine. Tommy is a pussycat, really." Well, not like Destiny, but I'd dodged that bullet for the day. No way was I bringing that up now. Hopefully, it would be a funny story to tell once we had the spell reversed, and I was back to being magic-less.

"Are there any other pointers from your classes you think might help us?"

I was coming up blank, so I just went with a shrug and a headshake. "Can you think of anyone you've pissed off lately? More than usual, I mean."

She gave me one of her looks. That was more like the Opal I knew and feared. Somehow, it made me feel better.

"Not to the point they'd want to kill me over it. I mean striking a hard bargain over an antique piece of furniture isn't exactly a motive for murder."

"Well, if you think of anything, let me know. So far I've pretty much ruled out Calvin Brenton."

She raised an eyebrow. "You thought it might involve him? Why?"

"Well, that was back when we thought they'd killed who they meant to kill. Valerie Kimble. From what I understand, she put the kibosh on a big hotel deal he was working on. But then he pointed out that you'd most likely replace her, and he'd be right back where he started from. Same would hold true now, I guess."

Opal looked thoughtful. "There's a thought. Maybe whoever is behind this wanted both of us dead. That deal would have meant a lot of money in the pockets of Calvin's backers. And yes, Calvin's pockets too." She gave me a thoughtful nod. "Good work, there, Amie. You might just have found your true calling."

I was speechless. Getting praise from Aunt Opal wasn't something I was used to. But I had to push that to one side. I could savor it later when time permitted. Because right now, I had work to do.

Opal was right about one thing. Just because the killer had tried to kill her first, didn't mean that Valerie Kimble hadn't been next on their list.

Chapter 17

I wanted to talk with Misty Rhodes again. She knew more than she'd been telling me. A lot more. I was kind of hoping that I could use the leverage of knowing about her and Calvin's affair to get the truth out of her. If that made me a bad person, so be it. I wanted to get to the bottom of this before the killer tried again.

But I had another talk ahead of me before I got to Misty. I had promised Aunt Opal to have a chat with Tommy Hill. Truthfully, I really thought it was a huge waste of time as Tommy wasn't the killer. A promise is still a promise, though.

Goddess help me, but if I hadn't still been in my pajamas, I'd have left right then and there without going back upstairs. I had no idea if Destiny was up yet or not, and I really didn't want to have to deal with two problems at the same time. Maybe he would agree to a truce until we caught whoever was out to kill Opal? It was worth asking. After all, it seemed like he still needed a place to hide out from his crazy ex-girlfriend. This would just be killing two birds with one stone, wouldn't it?

I took the stairs as quietly as I could. If I could make it to my apartment, get dressed, and make it to my car without Destiny knowing, then that was what I was going to do. Like I said, one problem at a time. Right now, my highest priority was keeping my family safe. I was pretty sure, though, that Destiny wouldn't feel the same way. Tough.

Pulling out one of my dressier sweatshirts—and yes, to me they can be dressy—I tugged it over my head and then finished the outfit with a pair of black jeans. I debated between my boots and my sneakers for a while, but the sketchers won out. They were just more comfortable. Besides, who knew if I'd need to run today? If I did, I wanted to be ready.

I thought I had made it, but just as I opened the door onto the balcony, Ruby's door opened.

"Going out, are we?"

Taking a deep breath, I turned to face him. "No, we are not. I am, though."

He smiled at me. "Don't worry, I wasn't going to try to go with you. Not dressed like this." He motioned down to his cut off sweats and girly T-shirt. Can't say I blamed him for that. "I was rather hoping you'd do me a favor, though."

A favor for my familiar? Well, I did owe him. "What's the favor?" I'm not stupid. I wasn't going to say yes until I knew what it was.

He hesitated. "First, would you tell me where we are?"

"Wind's Crossing, Michigan. Just outside of town actually. This is our farmhouse."

"Ah, so we're in Michigan." He nodded to himself. "That's good, actually." Then he turned his attention back to me. "Does this town of yours have a thrift shop of some kind? That maybe sells used clothes?"

I grinned at him. "Let me guess, you want a new wardrobe?"

His smile went lopsided. It looked sweet, actually. "In the worst possible way."

Was it awful that I had to think about it first? I mean, having clothes would give him a sense of freedom. What was to stop him from just taking off? Was there some kind of boundary that a familiar couldn't cross? Did they have to stay within a certain radius of their witch? There was so much I didn't know.

Then I realized, that at this point it really didn't matter. If he wanted to run, he could. In fact, that might just be the best thing that could happen right now.

"I'll see what I can find. What size do you wear?" I jotted down his sizes, including shoe size, and stuck the note in my pocket. "Is there anything else you want from town?" Within reason, but that went without saying. It wasn't like he'd had somewhere to carry a wallet. He was dead broke.

"Some food would be nice. You girls sure don't believe in stocking your refrigerators." He paused. "And would you mind if I borrowed your computer today? There's some stuff I need to check on back home."

I hesitated, then reached back and unlocked the door. "Help yourself. Just make sure you keep one of those noise barrier spells going wherever you are, okay? It wouldn't do for Opal to call the police because she heard someone walking around up here. I'm pretty sure a man makes more noise than a cat does."

He nodded. "Duly noted. I'll keep them both active for the immediate future."

I gave him one last nod and then headed down to my car. I was outside the Hill's residence within minutes. Oh, the never-ending joy of having four wheels and a motor.

I really wished that Tommy had his own place, but that wasn't the case. At least the last I knew, he still lived with his mom and dad. His dad, George, I could handle. He was nice enough if a bit of a pervert for spying on our skyclad coven meetings. His mother, however, was a very different story.

131

My luck was running as usual, and it was Naomi Hill that answered the door. I put on my brightest smile. It was hard in front of all that active hatred, but I did it.

"Hello, Mrs. Hill, is Tommy home?"

She growled at me. And yes, I'm being literal here. An actual growl. "No, he isn't, as if you didn't already know that. And if you aren't off my front steps in three seconds, I'm setting the dog on you."

Yeah, I knew Tommy's dog. That didn't scare me so much. "Can you give me a number where I might reach him?"

"Three, two…"

I didn't figure I would get any help from her. And the evil smile that came over her mouth as she started to say the word one made me rethink sticking around. Even though I'd already jumped down off her steps, she still gave the command.

The dog that rounded the corner into her entry and through her front door most definitely wasn't cuddly little Benny. It was a Doberman. Sleek, black, and extremely fast.

I must have broken a few track records making it back to my car but there was no time left to actually open the door and climb in. With a mighty leap, I jumped onto the hood and then clambered up onto the roof of the car. Hopefully, the Doberman wouldn't follow suit. I was cursing the fact that I'd left my taser at home. If I was going to continue in this line of work, I needed to get a holster for it and make it an everyday carry.

The dog lunged at the side of the car, but at least he didn't follow me up. I waited for Mrs. Hill to call him off, but that didn't happen. Instead, she gave a full, deep belly laugh and went back inside and closed the door.

Now, what was I going to do? My cell phone was sitting on the dashboard of my car, well out of reach. I winced as I heard the dog's nails scraping the metal of my car door. There was no question what would happen should he actually be able to reach me.

I was gathering myself up to scream when I heard Tommy call my name. Looking back, I saw him running toward me, two plastic bags of stuff in his hand. They were somewhat flying in the breeze of his run.

"Leo, down!" The dog gave one more lunge and snarl, throwing in a little extra drool this time, and then complied. He sat by the car, growling at me. It was an improvement, but still not an ideal situation.

Tommy grabbed his collar and then realized he couldn't handle the dog and the bags too. He handed the sacks to me and then got a good hold on the collar and dragged the huge beast back to the house. Once Leo was safely inside, Tommy came back.

"Let me guess. You came looking for me, and Mom set Leo on you."

"Got it in one." What was the best way to get off the roof of a car? Getting up was done in such a rush that I hadn't had time to stop and think about it. Getting down, with a handsome eyewitness standing right there, was a different story. Eventually, I sat down and kind of slid down the windshield to the hood. From there it was easy peasy. "She really doesn't like me."

He rubbed the back of his neck with one hand as he reached up and took the two bags I'd left on top of the car with the other. "No, she doesn't. But it isn't really you she hates." He hesitated. "Well, not at first it wasn't, anyway."

I started to ask what had changed that, but then I thought about the whole bounty hunting thing. That was probably enough to take me from extreme dislike over to the hate side of her list.

"Is there somewhere—away from here—that we could go to talk for a few minutes?"

His eyes lit up. "Sure. Let me take these inside and I'll be right back. I've got a new place, and we can go there."

As he took the few steps to the house, I hurried up and got into my car. Once that front door opened, there was always a chance that Leo would come barging out.

He didn't, and a couple of minutes later Tommy returned. "I told Mom if she ever set Leo on you again, the free groceries would stop." He shrugged. "It might not work but at least I tried."

I opened the car door, still looking warily at the front door. "Thanks for that. So do you live far?"

"Nope. Just down the block. Mr. Peterson is letting me rent out the loft in his garage. It's actually nicer than it sounds. A little one-bedroom apartment with a bathroom and everything. Kind of like your place, just smaller."

I wasn't quite sure how to approach the subject. I wasn't used to interviewing friends as possible suspects. Wasn't used to interviewing suspects when you got right down to it. So I figured I'd just approach this is a friendly conversation.

"I've been wondering why you showed up to that coven meeting the other night. I mean, you had to know it would drive your mom up the wall, right?"

The hand went to rubbing the back of his neck again. "Yeah, well, I was hoping she wouldn't find out."

I grinned at him. "Am I to assume it didn't work out that way?"

"That's the way to take it all right. And boy was she pissed off at me." He shuddered. "I was really glad I'd moved out by then. She can get downright mean when she's angry."

He didn't have to tell me that. Normal people didn't set a dog on you that would gleefully tear you to shreds.

"So, why did you go? Are you that interested in becoming a witch?"

The color rose in his cheeks. "Not exactly. It's just that… man, this is hard. I'm gonna come right out and say it, okay? I like you. I always have. Back in school, it was more of a crush actually, but back then, I was the Fat Geek. No way would someone like you give me the time of day."

What the heck? Fat Geek, also known as Hot Geek and Tommy Hill, had a crush on me? How did I not know that? Of course, finding it out now with this thing starting to bud toward Opie wasn't the best in the way of timing.

"As I remember it, we spent quite a lot of time together in school, actually."

"Yeah, but that was just because Opie invited me along whenever you guys hung out." He took a deep breath. "I'd have given anything if, just once, you were the one that called me."

We walked a few steps in silence. Then I remembered something. "Wait a minute, that night you said you didn't know it was a joint meeting. If that was true, you wouldn't have known I'd be there, right?"

The color deepened. "I wasn't there for you. Not in that way. I mean, I knew from my dad that full moon coven meetings were always in the nude. I'm not sure I would have stuck it out even if the grand argument hadn't erupted. That's not how I want it to go the first time you see me naked."

Now I could feel the heat rising in my cheeks too. Tommy had plans for me to see to him naked? And just like that, my thoughts totally derailed.

"I just know how important your craft is to you. I thought if I went to a meeting, I could see what it was all about. I asked Valerie for an invitation over a month ago." He made a face. "I don't think she would have given it at all if it hadn't been for the numbers. From what I gather, once Opal invited her coven for the full moon, they needed one more to make thirteen."

That sounded about like Valerie. Witches without true power were always trying to up their reach. It rarely ended well. Case in point.

We talked for a little while, and he took me on a short tour of his little space. It was pretty cool, even if it was just one large room with a separated bathroom. Like mine, space only allowed for a small shower stall. No bubble baths for the naked Hot Geek, either.

Obviously, my thoughts had not quite made it back on the tracks yet.

When I left him half an hour later, it was with my heart sure of his innocence.

But then again, my heart had been steering me wrong for years. Telling me guys didn't like powerless witches like me, when I'd had two admirers this whole time.

What did it know?

Chapter 18

My next stop was at the Thrift Store, where Destiny made out like a bandit. I didn't do so bad either. I left there with the cutest little cardigan and handbag for me, and two bags full of stuff for him.

His new wardrobe consisted of a pair of blue jeans, a pair of khakis, a button up dress shirt, two T-shirts, and a polo shirt. The only shoes they had in his size were of the flip-flop variety, but I figured it was slightly better than going barefoot, so I got them too.

The last item would only be his temporarily. I was totally taking it back when he left. I'd lucked into the buy of a lifetime: a short soft leather jacket with silky lining. I like my jackets big, so it would be a perfect addition to my wardrobe once Destiny was done with it. He'd better take good care of it.

After that, I went to the grocery and loaded up on food. Well, I got enough for a day or two. For me, that was stocking up. I'm a buy it as you need it kind of girl. At least now there would be the makings for sandwiches, and a couple of frozen family dinners for larger meals. And, of course, a frozen pizza. Can't go for long without my 'za.

With all the cold stuff, I then had to make a drop off at home before going to see Misty. That wasn't such a bad thing, as I was more than a little concerned just letting some strange man have full run of my living space. Periodic and sporadic check-ins would probably be a good thing for a while.

When I got home, Destiny was camped out on the sofa in my living room, my computer in his lap. Needless to say, he was in man form, not cat.

"Learn anything useful today?" I asked, trying to make light conversation. From his reaction, it didn't go over well.

"Like what?"

I shrugged. "Don't have a clue. Just wondering if you were able to find what you were looking for on the computer." I started to put the groceries away and then had a terrible thought. "You aren't doing anything illegal on my laptop, are you? I had a friend go to jail for that kind of thing." And I really didn't want to be next. What could I tell the cops? It wasn't me, it was my cat? Yeah, they'd put me in a loony bin for sure.

"Of course not! Just checking the local news back home, that's all. And some other things too. All perfectly legal, I promise." He shut the computer and laid it on the coffee table. "Do you need any help putting away the food?"

Dang, but he was sneaky. I hadn't even heard him walk up behind me. Maybe that carpet quiet spell worked just a bit too well.

"I've got it. There's cereal for breakfast and lunch meat and bread for quick lunches. I don't cook, so for evening meals, it'll be warmed up frozen dinners. The ones I get are pretty good. I hope you like Italian."

"Yum." He paused. "I don't suppose you had any luck at the thrift store then."

I snapped my fingers. "I knew I was forgetting something." When his face fell, I laughed. "In the trunk of my car, silly. I remembered the store, just forgot I'd put the bags in the trunk." He started out, but I laid my hand on his arm. "No way. Opal is still home. She isn't going to see a man in hoochie shorts coming down from my apartment, now is she?"

"No ma'am, but I would really like to get out of these... what did you call them?"

"Hoochie shorts. That's what my mom calls cut-offs. Probably because me and Ruby always cut them off a little shorter than Mom approved of." My stomach growled, and I realized I hadn't had breakfast yet, and here it was almost noon. "Make you a deal. I'll get the bags from the trunk if you make us a couple of sandwiches. I like ham the best, but turkey would work too."

"Deal."

I made the round trip in record time, but he was just as fast. By the time I made it back upstairs, there were three sandwiches cut in halves on a plate resting on the coffee table. I handed him his two bags and started stuffing my face.

He took a bite, then dumped the bags on the cushion next to him to sort through. "This is so cool. Thank you." Although when he got to the flip-flops, he just looked at me with his eyebrows raised.

"It was them or nothing. Next time I make it out of town to a department store I'll pick you up a regular pair of shoes. Here in Wind's Crossing the only shoe shop is out of my price range." Especially for a man with no money, even if he did happen to be my familiar.

"I don't suppose you figured out a way to break the binding spell?" I hated to bring it up, but it was a question I had to ask. But if I'd expected another sudden rush to anger, I didn't get one.

"Not yet, but I will." He was quiet for a minute as he finished his sandwich. "I'm hoping you'll let me stay here for a week or so anyway. Until I can figure some things out."

That didn't sound so very unreasonable. "I'm fine with that, but there will have to be rules. For one, can you alter the carpet quiet spell so that it only works to cover the noise you make? My friend, the deputy sheriff will be staying right below us and he's going to become suspicious if he doesn't hear anything."

He thought for a minute and then nodded. "I think I know a modification spell I can use that will work."

"Good." I polished off my sandwich and reached for half of the leftover one. "Split the last one?"

While we chewed, I tried to think of all the rules I had to have in place. I knew Ruby wouldn't want to give up her living space for a matter of weeks. One night, sure, a week or two, no way.

"If I can ask, why is the deputy sheriff staying here, anyway? Are you guys in some kind of trouble?"

I took a deep breath. It was only fair he knew what was going on. After all, if the killer tried something to take down the whole house and everyone in it, it would affect him just as well as us.

"You could say that." I didn't really want to go into details, so I just gave him the barest of details. "A lady, well a witch actually, that we know was murdered. As it turns out, the killer didn't mean to kill her. They meant to kill my aunt Opal."

I wasn't expecting his instant reaction or his loss of color.

"Wait a minute." Was it just me, or did his voice hold a certain element of panic? "You said we were in Wind's Crossing... and your aunt's name is Opal. Oh, my Goddess." He put his head in both his hands and leaned forward until his forehead almost touched his knees. "Please tell me your last name isn't Ravenswind."

And there I was yet again without my taser. I so had to get a holster for that thing.

"Are you going to freak out like you did last night if I say it is?"

He shook his head and groaned. "This is so bad."

Worse than being bound as another witch's familiar in what is possibly a lifetime spell? Come on. I mean, yes, Aunt Opal was a hardass, and she had a reputation among witches. But mostly they just respected her. There was nothing to really be afraid of, unless you were on the wrong side of the witch's council.

The witch's council. Why hadn't I thought of that before now? Could that have something to do with all this mess? The fact that Opal was a high-level witch on the council? And much more importantly right at this very moment, did the witch sitting across from me have anything to do with it?

I retrieved my taser and sat back down with it resting in my lap. He still hadn't moved. Well, if you didn't count the rocking back and forth as actual movement.

"Okay, I need you to tell me right now why being in Opal Ravenswind's house is such a bad thing. Are you on the council's bad side?" There, that was a much better start than 'Are you trying to kill my aunt?'.

At first, all I got was another, deeper groan. To me, that was answer enough. If the answer had been no, he would have said it right away.

My familiar wasn't just a witch.

He was a renegade.

Chapter 19

I couldn't do this alone.

Don't get me wrong. I wasn't afraid of him. Not with my taser in my lap, anyway. The instant he started chanting or making his fingers dance, he'd be lying on the floor in his own drool.

But I still needed Ruby. Once again, my need centered around her ability to do magic. Funny, but I'd been hoping by now to be able to do my own. Of course, I'd still have to learn how to use it and memorize actual spells, but I'd really hoped to be a lot farther along than I currently am.

Which happens to be still with no magic of my own. And I wasn't sure how drawing power from Destiny would work when he was awake. Could he stop me? Made sense that he could but it was a question for Ruby, anyway.

Not what I currently needed her for, however. What I needed right now was that truth spell she'd mentioned using on the married guy from her singles' retreat. Whatever story came out of Destiny's mouth, I wanted to know it was the truth.

He panicked when he saw me pick up my cell phone. "Who are you calling? Your aunt?"

I tilted my head at him. Men could be so silly sometimes.

"No, if I wanted Opal all I'd have to do is scream. She's right downstairs, you know." Although now I thought about it, with that darn carpet spell in place, she probably wouldn't hear me. Maybe I was the silly one here. "I'm calling Ruby to ask her to come straight home from work."

I wasn't about to tell him why. People generally don't enjoy being forced to tell the truth against their will.

She picked up on the first ring. "Hey Amie, I was just thinking about calling you. Got the sense you might need me." That wasn't unusual actually as it happened between us a lot. We were closer than twins in some respects, even if we did have different mothers.

We'd been bound by magic while still in the womb. One of the things in my life I was actually grateful for.

"Yeah, your spider sense was right on the nose. I was hoping you could come straight home when Opal relieves you at the shop today. I have need of that spell you used at the retreat."

She was instantly on board. "I knew he was hiding something big." There was a brief silence, and I just knew there was lip chewing going on. "Should I call Mom and ask her to come in early?"

"No!" Opal had a way of knowing things. If Ruby called her, she might jump to the obvious conclusion that I needed her. After reaching that conclusion, there would be one thing Opal would be certain to do. Come upstairs. That was the last thing we needed.

Well, until we found out exactly what was going on, anyway. After that, we might have to change our strategy.

The next three hours would pass by extremely slowly. I didn't know what was going on in his brain, but mine was working overtime. What had he done? The council didn't get involved in minor affairs. But if a witch used magic for evil? Well, they came down hard on that.

I had been kind of surprised we hadn't had a visit from the council when Valerie was found dead. The only reason that didn't happen was most likely that Opal had a seat on the board. Not an ordinary council member, my aunt. She never did anything halfway.

"I don't suppose you'd agree to go back to being a cat until Ruby gets here?" You couldn't blame me for asking. If he was a cat, I could shove him back in the carrier and lock it down tight. Couldn't really do that with a man.

He just looked at me. "What do you think?"

"Okay, so what do we do for the next three hours then? Just sit here and stare at each other? Sounds like fun."

"What would you have been doing if this hadn't come to light?"

"Interviewing a possible suspect."

His pupils narrowed and I could see his body stiffen. I moved my left hand up to my hair to distract him while my right hand inched toward the taser.

"You some kind of council cop or something?"

Even with the stress of the current situation, I laughed. I just couldn't help myself. Me, a council cop? It was far too funny for words. The council didn't even want to recognize me as a true witch, let alone give me any measure of responsibility. To them, I was just a useless screwup that couldn't hold down a job.

"That's rich, but no. I'm not affiliated with the council in any way, shape, or form." Well, except for being Opal's niece, but he already knew that.

"Then what are you?"

I shrugged. "Right now, I'm self-employed while I take online classes to get my private investigator license. Until I graduate, I pay what bills I have by taking on odd and end bounty hunting jobs and photography clients."

He smiled at me, some of his tension falling away. "Let me get this straight. You are a bounty hunter?" He chuckled. "You're what, all of five foot two?"

Straightening my back to its full extent, I gave him a glare. "I'm five feet and five inches, thank you very much." If I were wearing short heels, but that counted for me. "And I'll have you know that my last bounty hunter gig was taking down an ex-Special Forces fugitive."

Destiny didn't look so sure about that. "How much help did you have? Ruby cast a spell for you?"

Why did everyone always assume that?

"No, actually. I brought him in on my own. I'm not as useless as you and the bloody council might like to think."

His color returned in full force and brought friends. "Don't you dare link me with the bloody council. I have nothing to do with them and their highhanded self-righteous ways."

That would mean more to me if he wasn't on the run from them. As it was, it meant preciously nothing.

We stared at each other for a full minute or two. Then I repeated my question. "So, what do we do for the next three hours?" I was afraid I knew the answer to that one as it was staring me in the face. No way was I letting this man out of my sight until I got some answers.

"I could go with you to interview the suspect. Beats sitting around here and doing nothing."

Not going to happen and I told him so. "Sorry, but I don't trust you enough to go anywhere with you right now."

"Then why haven't you started interviewing me? If you're so good at it, I mean. Surely you'd be able to get to the truth of the matter in no time at all."

"I'm good at taking down bounty jumpers. I'm new to the whole interviewing process. That's why I want Ruby here."

He glanced around the room, then his eyes lit on my computer. "Mind if I continue my research while you sit and stare at me then? I do have things I could be doing."

So did I, but they would require the computer too. But then again, if I was working on the laptop, I couldn't keep a very good eye on him. That wasn't acceptable. I might not be a big fan of the council, but even I realized they did an important job.

It took some doing, what with the whole keeping him in sight the whole time thing happening, but I dragged out my little manual treadmill and yoga equipment. I could easily waste an hour or so by getting in a much-neglected exercise routine.

The only problem with that plan is that I don't exactly exercise in silence. But then that was his problem, not mine. I was fine with my grunts and groans.

After a few pointed glances my way, he finally got the hint that they weren't going to get me to stop what I was doing. Then he just went to ignoring me. I was cool with that too. It's not like I wanted a gorgeous man watching me sweat.

When I heard Opal leave to go relieve Ruby at the shop, a little of my tension left me. That was one less worry I had to deal with. Opal didn't make it a habit to come upstairs when just the two of us were home, but then she didn't normally seek out my advice on things, either. Today was a day of firsts.

After the sounds of her car faded away, I turned to Destiny. "Finish up what you're doing, then we're going for a walk. There are some things I need to gather from the woods, and I've elected you to hold the bag."

His look got wary, then calculating. "My bag holding depends. Would you be willing to share your spoils? I take it you are looking for spell ingredients?"

I nodded and thought about it. "I'll share, but it won't be fifty-fifty. House advantage."

"I'd agree to seventy-five to twenty-five, but that's as low as I'll go for bag holding duty."

"Agreed."

"Give me two minutes to change clothes?" His voice was hopeful.

It wasn't for the time, but for the opportunity to change. A part of me wanted to let him, but the smarter part of me won out. "Sorry, but until Ruby gets here you aren't getting out of my sight." I nodded to the clothes that were still sitting on the sofa beside him. "Knock yourself out but do it here."

He took a deep breath and then stripped to the skin and redressed in the new to him jeans and T-shirt. After all, I'd already seen him naked as a jaybird. That ship sailed last night.

"Could I make another small request when you finally make it to that supermarket?"

I grinned. I'd caught the wince he gave when he zipped up those jeans. "Underwear?"

"Yeah. Going commando isn't my thing."

We stuck close to home, for a couple of reasons. One was that I wanted to hear Ruby when she made it home. The other was that Destiny was wearing flip-flops. Not exactly appropriate footwear for hiking in the woods. Still, we made a pretty good haul. I was hoping the gift would put Opal in a better frame of mind. Woods gathering wasn't one of my favorite things to do.

Our timing was perfect, and as we made our way back to the farmhouse with a full sack of assorted mushrooms and plants, Ruby rode up on her bike. She looked relieved to see both of us together. Or maybe she was just relieved to see me.

Because she also looked worried as heck.

Ruby was complicated like that.

***

Once we had taken our places in my sitting room, I told him what the plan was. I'd expected him to balk, but he didn't. He did, however, have one stipulation.

"I'll agree to be put under a temporary truth spell, if you will allow me to not answer the questions I object to. If you think about it, it's only fair. You could literally ask me anything. I should have the right to refuse."

Ruby looked over at me and gave a slight nod. If she was okay with it, then so was I.

I saw Destiny's eyes glued on her as her hair began to float. She truly was a beautiful woman, but when she was casting a spell that beauty only magnified. Ruby was breathtaking.

When she finished, she took her seat beside me on the couch. Destiny was sitting in a chair in front of us. Proper interviewing style. And yes, my taser was within easy reach. I can be taught.

Ruby glanced my way. "Is it okay if I start things off?" I nodded.

She turned to Destiny and tilted her head. "Perhaps we should handcuff him first?"

He gave her a nasty smile. "You could try."

His confidence came across even with the truth spell in place. That wasn't a good sign. He had power, but then I'd already known that. Shoot, the two of us had grown an oak tree together. How many people could say that? And not mean over a period of decades?

Ruby flexed her fingers and sparks flew. Yeah, she had power too. And from the look of things, she'd been pulling magic for quite some time. I was getting more than a little worried. Magical wars were nothing to sneeze at, even if they were just between two witches.

"Before you two start a gigantic pissing match that we're all going to regret, should we live through it, why don't we just try talking?" As neither one of them looked like they were willing to take that advice, I upped my ante. "Or I could just taser both your butts and when you come to, you'd both be handcuffed."

That startled Ruby. "Hey, I'm trying to protect you here. You don't know who he is!"

Her words worked better than my taser threat. Destiny deflated right before our eyes. The magic was the first to go, then his shoulders slumped and finally, he dropped down into the chair.

"Maybe she's right." His head was once again in his hands. "If you want to handcuff me, so be it."

I gave Ruby a hard look. "Do you think it's really necessary?" It was obvious by this point that she had information about our house guest I didn't. From the look of it, it wasn't good news either.

Her teeth caught her lip as she stared at the man now slumped in the chair and back to doing his rocking thing. "Maybe not." Then in a side voice just for me. "But keep that gun of yours handy just in case."

Heck yeah. That was never not going to happen.

We sat back down, and I looked to Ruby. "You wanted to start things off. Go for it. Who is he?"

"Archimedes Mineheart, from the powerful Earth witch genealogical line. Pretty much the Earth magic equivalent to us Ravenswinds." Then she swallowed. Bad news coming up. "And he's wanted for questioning in the murder of his girlfriend, Sonya."

A glance at Destiny—Archimedes?—showed him still rocking.

"I didn't do it. And she wasn't exactly my girlfriend, but we dated off and on. I would never have hurt her. We might not have been a couple, but we were friends. Good friends. And I want to know who killed her. More than anyone, probably, and not just because it would clear my name, either."

Still rocking. Somehow that rocking more than anything convinced me he was telling the truth. Even more so than the fact that he was under Ruby's truth spell.

He was innocent. But that wouldn't stop the witch's council if they found out we were harboring a fugitive renegade in our home.

Eventually, they would find him.

And us.

Chapter 20

Ruby wanted to bring Opal into our little circle of knowledge, and I wanted nothing more than to agree with her. But wisdom won out and said no. Opal was on the council's board. Innocent man or not, she would be honor bound by her oath to the council to turn him over.

I didn't want that. The truth was, I liked him. Not in a romantic way, thank the Goddess, but there was just something about him that called to me. Something ethereal that linked us, even more so than the binding spell. Of course, it could just be the spell. I'd never had a familiar before. Perhaps this was just a natural extension of that.

Either way, I wanted to help him. Ruby wasn't happy keeping something this big from her mom, but as it was her truth spell that convinced us (well convinced her) that he wasn't a killer, she finally agreed.

"But I don't want you off running to Indiana with him trying to solve Sonya's murder. Not yet." Her voice softened. "We need you right now, Amie."

After all those years of having to go to them whenever I was in trouble, those words were more precious than gold to me. For once in my life, I was on the right track. I could help them instead of being the one needing help. No way would I desert them. Not even for my new familiar.

We'd have to solve our little problem first. I was just really surprised when I found out that Destiny—I mean Archimedes—was more than okay with that.

"Look, I can't bring Sonya back, so rushing back there right now wouldn't solve anything other than giving the council a better shot at nabbing me. Right now, I can do what I need to on the computer." He paused. "I'd offer to help you guys too, but…"

"That would not be a good idea," Ruby said. "You will have to lay very low for a while."

He nodded. "I know, but if there is anything I can do from here, let me know, okay?"

"Actually, there is." Both of them looked at me. "Well, there are times when all of us are gone, right? That would be the perfect time for the killer to come in and lie in wait or, I don't know, plant a bomb or something. Archimedes here can act as our watchman."

"I could do that. And you two can call me Arc. All my friends do."

"Arc it is. Now I have someplace I need to be, so do you two promise to play nice with each other while I'm gone?"

Ruby just gave me the look. "I'm taking Yorkie for a nice long walk." She glanced at Arc. "Sorry I can't invite you along."

I was about to ask her why not, as Opal was still at the shop for a few hours, then the sound of tires on gravel reminded me. Opie.

To save the hassle of hiding Arc, I went to meet him at his car, then walked into Mom's apartment with him. He'd brought a couple more bags. Looked like he was planning to stay for a while.

We made small talk for a few minutes and then I broke it to him. "I'm going to talk with Misty Rhodes again."

That got his attention.

"I'm assuming it has to do the murder investigation." The way he said it, it wasn't a question.

"Yup. Opal said something this morning that got me thinking. That hotel deal means a lot of money to a lot of people. Everyone knows Calvin isn't happy in his marriage, but it's his wife that has the money. If the deal goes through, it could open the door to him getting a divorce."

He gave a slow nod. "And maybe make it official with Misty. But that still doesn't explain why they went after Opal. And we'd pretty much already cleared him on the Valerie case."

"We had. But what if they fully intended to kill both of them? Opal and Valerie both stood in their way. Who is to say that this was just a one murder thing? Maybe they'd planned for two."

"And the killer just got the second intended victim first by accident?"

I nodded. "A happy little coincidence for them that it still hit home if we're right."

"One more question. You keep saying 'they'. Do you think Calvin and Misty are in this together?"

Good question. "You have to admit, it's possible. But it could just be one or the other of them too." I paused. This was the part I really didn't like. "Or it could be one of his investors. That would open up the possibility of a lot more suspects."

"True, but if we're following the money, Calvin definitely had the most to lose with that deal not going through. He's not likely to get more investors any time soon. His career as a high-powered deal maker is pretty much done if this hotel thing doesn't work out."

"Even more reason to take out the two witches standing in his way."

"Give me a minute to change out of uniform? Our visit to Misty might go better if I'm not dressed up as the law."

I grinned at him. "I don't recall inviting you along."

"Oh, I'm going. The only question is whether or not we take separate cars."

"Go change, I'll start the car and drive around front to pick you up."

He hesitated. "We can take my car. I brought my personal vehicle tonight in case we wanted to go somewhere." His cheeks reddened as he said it, making me curious as to what he had planned.

"You don't want to be seen in my car, do you?"

His laughter kind of answered that for me. "Two minutes and I'll be ready."

I was tempted to time him, but more than likely he could do it. Men had it easy when getting ready. I doubted he'd even take the time to brush his hair. Which reminded me. I hadn't even changed after my workout. A quick sniff of my armpits and I was running back upstairs.

Five minutes later I was freshly dressed, complete with applied deodorant. My hair was even sparkling and untangled. Go me.

Opie was waiting at the bottom of the stairs. "Guys win again."

I stuck my tongue out at him. "Did you even comb your hair?"

His hand instantly ruffled through it. "Does it need it?"

Well, it did now, but I just shook my head. Guys would be guys. It wouldn't matter to him much even if I said yes. Besides, he'd comb it and then his hand would dishevel it again in no time. It was no wonder why he didn't bother.

A short drive later, he pulled up and parked across the street from Misty's, and we stared at the house for a while. The kids were playing out front—some kind of badminton type game. All I knew was that they were awfully heavy-handed with their rackets.

"Let's do this." I opened my car door but then I noticed Opie still hadn't moved.

"Maybe we should wait until tomorrow when the kids will be in school."

"Look, you aren't in uniform, so this isn't an official visit. We're just friends dropping by for a little chat."

"If you say so." He watched the kids for a little longer. "Okay, as long as the kids stay out here, I'm okay with this."

Good, because with or without him, I was going in. But it would be nice to have a ride back home.

Misty didn't seem at all surprised to see the two of us on her doorstep. She threw open the door and walked down her short hallway without even saying a word.

Opie and I shared a look and then closed the front door and followed her. We ended up in her living room. She was already curled back up on the sofa when we got there, a glass of wine in her hand.

"I'd offer you guys a glass, but this is the last of it." She held up the glass and drank. "I figured it was fitting to drink my last bottle of wine tonight. I'd been saving it, but no reason to anymore."

"Has something happened?" I asked that because it looked like maybe she'd drunk the entire bottle in a fairly short amount of time. She was pretty wasted. That accounted for her list to the right coming down the hall.

"You could say that." Misty glared at me and then Opie. "It's partly you two's fault, you know."

"What on earth did we do?" So far, I was the only of my dynamic duo that was doing any talking. Opie probably saw Misty as a woman in distress and was about to go into shining knight mode. He was known for that.

"Well, for starters, you practically found me and Calvin together. And don't try to pretend you didn't know I was there. I saw you two sitting in that car as I drove past."

"But we never told a soul. What goes on behind closed doors isn't anything to be spreading around town." Finally,

Opie joined the conversation. Sure, when he was saying something to try to help.

"Doesn't matter if you told or not, it put the fear of getting caught into him. He broke it off. Now, I got nobody."

Well, technically she had her kids, right? But I know a lot of women don't feel complete without a man. Personally, I've never understood that, but I've been around long enough to know it's true.

She took another big swig and then cradled the glass in her hands, the liquid inside sloshed about dangerously close to the edge. "We had it all planned out. He'd make a boatload of money off the hotel deal, and then we'd sell this place and move over to Big Spring or someplace nice and start over. After the divorce was final, of course."

Opie looked conflicted. I could tell he wanted to press her for information, but his white knight syndrome was getting in the way. Good thing I didn't have a problem with that.

"Sounds like getting that hotel through was a bigger deal than I thought for Calvin." Then I lowered my voice and glanced around like we were conspirators or something. After all, he had just broken up with her. She had no reason to protect him any longer. "Do you think maybe he wanted the deal a little too much and decided to do away with Val and Opal?"

"Opal?" Her eyes widened. "Is she dead now too?" Then the giggles started. "Shoot, if only he'd held out with me a little longer…" Then her eyes got a calculating look in them. Well, as calculating as they could look as watery and unfocused as they were from the drinking. "I told him I'd get things to work out one way or another, but the fool didn't believe me."

Okay, so that sounded an awful lot like a confession to me. Then she set the glass down and reached into a drawer in the table beside her. "If you two hadn't gotten in the way…"

I didn't wait for her to finish that sentence. I'd seen countless movies and read a ton of books that featured this kind of scene. It never ended well for the detective, amateur or not. The villain confessed to the crime and then pulled a gun. A quick dive and I was behind the easy chair and out of the line of fire.

And once again, I'd left my taser at home. I blame the over confidence that having Opie with me gave me. This was so his fault. If he'd stayed in uniform, he'd have had his sidearm.

That's when I realized that he was still just standing there. I was thinking about tackling him to the ground before the bullets started flying when I realized he was grinning down at me.

"What is wrong with her?" Misty's voice sounded garbled.

Opie glanced back at her. "I think maybe she lost an earring. She has a tendency to do that kind of thing when she feels one slip off."

What was he talking about? Taking a huge risk, I popped up just enough to see over the back of the chair. No gun. Instead, Misty just sat there, dabbing at her eyes with a tissue.

Opie leaned down and whispered, "Do you need a bag?"

I glared at him. "No, I don't need a bag." I stood up with my fingers to my earlobe. Hopefully, that would give a little support to Opie's outright fib.

Opie's grin faded as he glanced from Misty to the front door. "Do you need help with the kids tonight?"

The very fact that he offered when I didn't even think about it humbled me. Trevor Opie Taylor was a good man. I'd always known that, of course, but now the blinders were coming off big time.

She shook her head. "My sister is staying here for a while, at least until I get my head on straight. If I can't work things out with Calvin, who knows? We might move back home so I can be closer to her. It isn't like it would inconvenience my ex or anything. He isn't much of a father." Then the sobs started in earnest.

Grabbing my arm, Opie pulled me to the door. "We're done here."

Once in the car, I looked at him. "She as much as confessed, didn't she? Why aren't you calling your dad right now?"

"I'll admit she's a desperate woman, but I just don't think she's our killer. Right now her heart is broken, and she needs time to rebuild. Hopefully one day, she'll come to realize that the dirtbag that is Calvin Brenton never intended to marry her. She's pretty smart. I think she'll get there."

"But she'd do anything to win him over. I'm thinking that includes murder. As you said, she's a desperate woman. They do things like that." Plus she had laughed—actually laughed—when she thought Opal had been killed too. There was something very wrong with that.

He shrugged. "We'll keep her name on the list of suspects for sure, but I think you need to widen your suspect pool a little." He hesitated. "Want to grab a pizza while we're out? My treat."

It was so tempting. But there was a little guilt in the back of my mind. If I was going to eat pizza, I should order in so I could share with Ruby and Des—I mean, Arc. Then, of course, he said the magic words.

"Carnie's Pizzeria okay with you?"

The man knew my weaknesses and wasn't above exploiting them.

"We could even, I don't know, maybe talk about the case while we ate?"

Okay, now he really wasn't playing fair. Besides, I reasoned, I had stocked the fridge and freezer just today. The two of them could fend for themselves.

"Extra cheese?"

"Was that ever not an option?"

Sometimes, I loved this man.

Wait, what?

Chapter 21

He kept his word, but we didn't come up with any startling new revelations on the case. Mostly that was because we were too busy stuffing our faces. It was Carnie's after all. The best pizza joint in the entire state of Michigan, possibly the world.

After we ate, we sat at the table and nursed our sodas. Still, no grand ideas or theories came to mind. I was still convinced this had something to do with that hotel deal. He wasn't so sure.

There was one thing that was bothering me, though.

"How does one go about poisoning a donut? I mean, I'm pretty sure Mr. Clark didn't poison the whole batch or there would be more deaths in town. And I watched the whole time he bagged my purchase. When did it get poisoned, and how?"

Opie picked up a tiny piece of crust left on the pizza plate, the entire remains of our dinner, and popped it in his mouth. "I'm not sure about the when, but I can make a strong guess on the how. All you'd need is a syringe to inject it right into the center."

"But you can't just go into a store and buy syringes, can you? Don't you need a prescription for that kind of thing?"

"Well, yeah, if you want one that hasn't been used." His eyes traveled over the now totally empty pizza plate looking for another scrap we'd missed. Like that was a possibility. "But if I needed a needle to use for something like this, I could find one pretty easily. I mean, all it would take would be a trip to the emergency room at the hospital on some made up ailment. Once you were alone in the room, a quick look into the disposal container labeled 'sharps' would probably give you enough ammunition for a half dozen murders."

Dang, that was scary. One that it was true, and two that he could come up with it.

I was opening my mouth to ask a follow-up question when Opie's cell phone went off. As the ringtone was the song, *I Shot the Sheriff*, I could only guess it was his dad calling.

"Hey, Dad, what's up." There was a pause as his eyes flashed to me. "I'm at Carnie's with Amie, why?" Another pause, a more worrying one this time as his face changed. The man sitting across from me was no longer off duty.

Even worse, from the look he was giving me, I just knew it had to do with my family. I was about ready to demand to know what was going on when he ended the call and stood up.

"Time to go. There's trouble at the farmhouse."

By the time we got there, the front parking spaces were completely filled with police vehicles and a large, bright red firetruck. I jumped out of the car before Opie even got it parked, stumbled, and then ran around to the front door.

Once inside and I saw Opal and Ruby talking with the sheriff, my heart relaxed. Then I saw the damage. I hadn't even noticed it from the outside. My mind had been too distracted by the fate of my family. Now that I knew they were okay, it hit me hard.

Both big picture windows, the ones in both my mom's and Opal's apartments had been shattered. But that was only the starter. In Opal's sitting room, the damage from the fire had been contained fairly quickly. Although, from the look of the chair if she'd been sitting there, things would have gone very differently. The chair would not survive this.

My eyes flew to Bridget's cage and perch. She was silent, which wasn't like her at all, but she didn't seem to be harmed. Then I stepped into my mom's place.

Normally things like this would send me into hyperventilation mode, but not this time. I wasn't scared or upset. I was angry. Nail spitting, jewel kicking, tear their hair out angry.

I felt Opie's presence behind me as I walked through her living room. The fire had gotten a short chance to take hold here, and it showed. Mom would have to replace more than just a chair and a window.

The hand-woven rug that she'd made years ago in her crafty phase, the crocheted doilies my grandmother had made that rested on the coffee and end tables, and most, if not all, the furniture in the room was damaged beyond repair.

And something really weird happened. My hair started floating. All on its own. I wasn't calling magic, but it was flooding into me, anyway.

Which created another thing to worry about. I had to find a safe way to release it. If I knew who was responsible for this, I would have no problem sending a massive karma spell their way. As it was, I had no easy outlet to use.

A soft meow behind me had me whirling. Destiny was standing at my feet. When he knew he had my attention, he leaped. I caught him in midair. In my arms, he lifted up onto his hind legs so that his green eyes could search mine. He looked worried.

With good cause. I was freaking out more than a little. Then even more strangeness started in. Not that what I was experiencing already wasn't strange enough. But at least this was a little easier to take.

The magic started to ebb out of me and into him. I could tell, because by the time I was feeling myself again, every little hair on his entire body was standing on end. At which point he jumped down and ran out the still open front door.

"Should I go after him?"

Opie's question startled me. Not that he should ask, but because I had totally forgotten he was even there. It took me a minute to come back to the reality of my current situation.

"No, he'll be back."

"Will you be okay here if I go join the others?"

To hell with that. I was going too. I wanted to know exactly what had happened here and who to send one heck of a kick-ass spell to.

Sheriff Taylor was just finishing up with Opal when we came in. He looked up at Opie and nodded to me. "She okay?"

"Shocked, but yeah, I think so."

Normally I would get upset about little things like men talking about me as if I wasn't standing right there. Right now it didn't faze me one bit. I had more important things to be upset about. Like someone trying to kill my aunt. And just maybe all of us to boot.

I did something I've only done a handful of times in my whole life. I walked up to Opal and gave her a hug. Seconds later, Ruby joined in. We stayed like that for a moment, just gathering strength from each other and knowing that, for this minute in time, we were all safe.

"I'd like for you three to check into a hotel somewhere for a while." The sheriff was back. Opie standing right behind him.

Our hug ended, and we were all standing a little taller because of it. We were Ravenswinds, dash it all. We would survive this and anything else a mere mortal threw our way.

"I appreciate that, sheriff, but I'm not leaving my home. If we hadn't been here tonight, we would have lost everything."

"No. You would have lost your house, which is insured, and your possessions which are replaceable." He laid a gentle hand on her shoulder and turned her toward her favorite chair, the one that didn't survive. "If you had been sitting there, you would have lost everything. There is a difference."

I swallowed. He was right about that, and it scared the daylights out of me. Even ultra-powerful witches will burn when flames touch them. Just look at our rather sordid history.

She shook her head. "I'm not leaving." Then she looked over at the window and blew out a long breath. "But we will need to do something about the windows before we go to bed tonight."

"I've already made a call about that. Billy Myers should be here shortly with some plywood and tools to get you fixed up temporarily. I'd still feel better if you'd go somewhere else for a night or two, but I understand."

"Thank you, Sheriff." Then she looked over at Opie. "You're more than welcome to stay, but I'm afraid staying in Sapphire's apartment isn't such a good idea. The smoke and water damage will have to be cleaned up before anyone will be comfortable there."

He gave me a questioning glance. I know what he wanted. He was hoping I'd offer the couch in my apartment. God and Goddess, but my life was getting too complicated. Having him here would be good, but I couldn't really ask Arc to stay in Destiny form for the duration of his visit. Wouldn't be fair.

"I'm thinking maybe we should bring over the tent and have us a front yard camp out."

I don't know if the sheriff could read my expression or if he'd already had that thought. Either way, I was grateful.

"A tent has thinner walls, and we'd be able to hear someone coming easier."

Opie looked disappointed, but he nodded. "Now that the killer seems to have upped their game, having two of us here might not be such a bad idea at that." He gave one of his crooked grins. Had they always been that sexy? "A man's gotta sleep sometime."

Opal gave them a smile. "That would be right nice of you two."

And if would have been too, if only I wasn't harboring a fugitive wanted in an active murder investigation upstairs. Things could get very interesting over the next few days.

Chapter 22

As Opie already had most of his stuff here—thank goodness he'd stashed his bags back in the bedroom and not the living room—the sheriff was the one that went to collect the tent and their sleeping bags. That would give him the opportunity to pack a light bag for himself.

Opal had already pulled out her extra keys and given each of the men one of their own. If you can't trust the law, who can you trust, right?

I have to admit that while I was grateful for the sheriff's offer, it did make me wonder as to why he made it. Opie, I could understand. We were close. Real close. Kindergarten on close, him and us. But camping out on someone's front lawn was a stretch any way you looked at it for a sheriff's duty.

Funny thing was, Opal didn't seem to think his offer all that odd at all. Almost like… she expected it or something. What with finding out about her history as a heart breaker with George Hill, it had me thinking that maybe there was a history somewhere between her and the sheriff. After all,

169

she's the only one I've ever heard call him by his given name. And as his wife had left him years ago, the man was more than fair game. Orville and Opal, kind of had a nice ring to it when you stopped to think about it.

Which I most definitely didn't have the time to do right now. No, now I had to find a reason to ditch Opie long enough to find Arc and see if he had anything important to tell us. Like maybe if he saw who threw those firebombs.

My chance finally came when Billy got there to do the temporary repairs on the windows. Billy was a little slow, but he was a good and dependable worker as long as the job in question didn't make him think too much. This was a straightforward job. One he could do easily. All of us townsfolk kept an eye out for jobs like that he could do. He was a good man.

With Opie recruited to help hand him tools and supplies while he worked, Ruby and I set out after Arc. Opal was busying herself trying to determine the extent of the damage to Mom's stuff. I hoped it wasn't as bad as I feared, but fire and water can do some nasty things.

We finally found him lying under a big maple tree that I didn't remember from oh, this morning. Crap. Opal wouldn't miss something this big. How were we supposed to explain that? As usual, Ruby read my mind.

"Let's worry about the repercussions of the instant tree later, okay?"

I nodded. She had my vote.

Bending down, I checked on Destiny. He was breathing, but it wasn't an even thing. Instead, his breath was coming in gasps.

"He funneled an awful lot of magic off you, didn't he?"

"Yeah." He was still conscious, and that was a good thing. I'd fainted after I made the oak tree. Then again, he had years of experience with this kind of thing. I was still new to it. "Hey, Arc, you okay?"

He lifted his head, but it took a real effort on his part. That was all I needed to see. I scooped him up into my arms and carried him inside and to the steps. There, Ruby hesitated.

"Look, I want to go with you, but…"

"Your mom needs you more right now. I'd feel the same way if things were reversed. You take care of Opal, and I'll take care of Arc."

Once upstairs, I locked my bedroom door and laid him on the bed. "You can change now. It's safe."

He slowly shook his head, then started softly snoring. The magic had really taken a toll on him. More so than I'd originally thought. I gave him a few minutes, while I went into the kitchen to make two quick cups of chamomile tea. I wasn't sure what the proper type of tea was for this kind of situation, but it just seemed right.

When I made it back into the bedroom, Arc was back in human form. I quickly threw a blanket over him then gently shook his shoulder. He started awake and bolted into a sitting position.

His eyes were wide with horror as he stared at me. "What the heck are you?"

I frowned at him. "What do you mean what the heck am I? I'm an air witch, though not a very good one." I hesitated. "I'm sorry I pulled that much power from you again. I really wasn't trying to."

His head tilted and his brows drew together. "What the devil are you talking about? I pulled the power from you not the other way around. Otherwise, it would be you lying here weak as a—I can't believe I'm going to actually say this— kitten."

That couldn't be right, but I just didn't have time to go into that now. "As interesting as that take on things might be, I think we need to concentrate on what happened before that. Did you see anything? Like who throw those Molotov Cocktails?"

His hand rubbed his forehead. Yeah, growing trees can give you a heck of a headache. I knew that from past experience.

"I saw something, all right, but I don't think you will like it."

I sat on the edge of the bed. "Give it to me."

"When I heard the glass break, I ran to the window overlooking the street."

That would be my bedroom window, but I couldn't exactly complain about that, considering the circumstances. "And?"

"And… I saw whoever it was threw those firebombs climb into a big blue car and take off down the driveway."

I was trying to be patient, I mean, I could understand that he didn't know the people around here. Still, not having to drag everything out bit by bit would sure save time. Especially as we now had an actual eyewitness.

"So what did they look like? Male, female, tall, short, what?"

"That's just it. I really couldn't tell you. First of all, all I caught was a glance, and it's hard to tell height from up above." He swallowed. "And it's hard to tell anything about someone wearing a coven robe."

That brought me up short. The Windsong Coven was the only coven around that I knew of that used ceremonial robes. I knew for a fact that you wouldn't find a single one in any of the Ravenswind closets. They just weren't necessary to get the job done.

If he'd told me this prior to our visit to Misty's I'd have sworn it sealed her fate. Now, it seemed to exonerate her. As inebriated as she had been when we left her, there wasn't any way on earth she could have driven herself here and done this.

But there were eight other members of the coven besides her that were still alive and well. And every one of them had a robe.

Then the thought that I really didn't want surfaced in the front of my brain.

Tommy Hill had one too.

***

We waited until everyone got settled in for the night. Opie and his dad were in a small tent off to the side of the front yard. It was a camouflaged model, so it wasn't likely to be seen unless someone already knew it was there. It blended especially well in the dark of the night.

Ruby came up after Opal finally shooed her away. My aunt wasn't one to like people hovering around her. It made her feel weak. Funny, but that was one word I would never use to describe Opal. She was absolutely the strongest woman I had ever known. If she were a little scared right now, well, all that proved was that she was human.

She gave a quiet tap on my bedroom door when she reached the landing and I let her in, then re-locked the door. Tired didn't even begin to describe the way she looked. I wasn't sure she was up to what me and Arc had planned.

Maybe we could manage it without her?

When she saw the mess in the living room, her shoulders slumped even further. "You're spell casting? At a time like this? Shouldn't you be spending your time trying to figure out who is doing this and why?"

Okay, that wasn't like my cousin at all, and her words stung. "Well, since my investigation has hit a snag, I thought maybe protecting my family would be something worthwhile to invest some time in." I knew she was hurting, but I couldn't keep the bitterness out of my voice. I was hurting too. "In case it has escaped your notice, we have a fairly powerful earth witch here."

Her eyes widened and her breath quickened. "You're working on wards?"

Don't get me wrong. Our farmhouse had wards. But the different elements of magic had different strengths. One of earth's magical strengths was protection spells. Air magic, not so much. Ours were okay, but nothing spectacular. At this point, I think we all wanted spectacular. I knew for a fact I did.

She sank down onto the sofa. "I'm sorry I snapped earlier. It's been a rough night. That was a really close call for Mom." A tear rolled down her cheek. "If she'd been sitting in her normal spot…"

My anger vanished as if it had never been. Sitting beside her, I pulled her in for a sideways hug. No words needed. They rarely were between the two of us.

When she had herself under control, she motioned toward the mess of powdered herbs on the table. "So what's all this then?"

Arc swelled by at least two inches. "This is the unbeatable ward my family perfected. It's never failed us yet." Then he lost his enlarged stature. "Or at least that was true until a few days ago." He took a deep breath. "It's still the strongest ward ever spelled, as far as I'm concerned. And one of these days very soon, I plan on finding out just how someone broke it."

That had to be involved somehow with Sonya's death, but I didn't want to ask. Not now, when we had important work to do.

Ruby was looking at the herbs with interest. If I knew my cousin, and I did, she was trying to place the recipe firmly in her head. Earth witches weren't known for sharing their spells. Neither were Air witches for that matter.

"There is a problem, though." I sucked in a deep breath. "Arc can't place the ward himself because of our guests. We have to do it."

She eyed the herbs a little longer. "This is a pretty large house with a heck of a lot of doors and windows. Is that going to be enough?"

"This is the active part of the spell, but we can mix it with another substance and then pour it in a thin line around the base of the house. That will take care of all the entrances, glass or wood."

"How does it work?"

"If the ward's boundary is breached by anyone with ill intent toward a resident inside, things will get loud. Fast."

"How loud? Opal is a pretty sound sleeper." Ruby was too, but she wasn't going to admit that.

"Fourth of July fireworks loud." He thought for a minute. "Now that I think about it, that's a good name for the spell. The Mineheart Fireworks' Ward. I kind of like that."

"Good, so what do we mix it with?" I was more interested in getting the ward in place than just sitting around naming it. I was still more freaked out about what had happened than I wanted to admit.

If the killer had waited only a few hours, we might have slept through the glass breaking and none of us may have survived the attack. Including Opie, who would have been front and center for the attack. That thought was bothering me a lot. He was putting himself in grave danger just being around us.

I didn't like that one bit.

"Well, it can't be liquid, so something grainy preferably."

"You mean like sugar?" Ruby asked. We knew salt was a no go. It had a bad influence on spellcraft. Well, unless it was one of the active ingredients, anyway.

Arc wagged his head back and forth. "Sugar might work, but how does your Mom feel about ants?"

Ah, yes, good point. Then I had one of my light bulb moments. "What about kitty litter?"

I mean, it wasn't like I had a use for it anymore, and I'd bought a really large bag. After all, a familiar binding was a lifelong thing. That was back when I had thought that was a good thing.

He nodded, and we made short work of combining the spell with the litter and then placing it in containers. Arc gave us a small example of how to lay the spell dust out, and Ruby and I got to work.

We'd barely made it down the staircase when Opie popped out of the trees to the right of the house and about gave me a heart attack.

"What are you girls doing?"

Ruby hefted the large mop bucket she was carrying. "We're laying down a protection ward."

Opie glanced around. "Would it be okay if I went with you?"

The two of us looked at each other. We'd planned on each taking a different direction around the house and finishing the job in half the time. More than likely that wouldn't happen now. We couldn't make Opie chose like that. And he couldn't very well be in two places at the same time.

Finally, I nodded, then smiled. "Sure. But you get to carry a bucket." Ruby and I could take turns with the remaining one.

There was barely enough to go around the house, but we made it work. It helped that the entire East side of the house only had windows on the second floor. We thought that would be the safest outside wall from the standpoint of an attack, so we laid the spell out there last. The ward line was thinner than the one that covered the rest of the house, but at least there was one.

When the last inch of the spell was laid, Ruby and I reached down and touched the line of powder. There was a brief white light that flashed over the house, from the bottom to the top and then disappeared.

I glanced at Opie. Was that visible to non-witches? His open mouth and wide eyes gave me my answer. He'd seen it all right.

"It's true, then. You girls really can do magic?"

He still doubted that, even after knowing us all this time? Then I thought about it. It probably wasn't all that weird after all. Magic was something you did in private, not in public with witnesses. Too many people still out there still had burn 'em at the stake mentalities.

I just gave him a hug. "Well, Ruby can." And Opal, and Mom. Just not me. Not unless I pull the magic out of Arc.

Opie walked us back to the outside stairs and watched as we climbed them. When we waved to him from the top, he disappeared back into the woods. It would be a long night for him.

Me? I was going to sleep.

And tomorrow I was going to visit every single member of the Windsong Coven until I found the one that was trying to kill my aunt.

Chapter 23

I woke up the next morning and made my list first thing. Eight coven members to check out. Then I realized that it might be fairly easy to rule some of them out right off the bat by finding out what color of car they drove.

It wouldn't be perfect, but it could narrow the field down and help me get where I wanted to go just that much faster. And yes, I wanted to tell Opie and his dad about what Arc had seen, but I didn't know how. Ruby and Opal had been too preoccupied with putting out the fires to see anything, and what was I supposed to say? My cat saw it? Yeah, that would go over real big, wouldn't it?

It didn't take long to look up the coven members' addresses on the computer. With my list in hand, I got ready for the day. A quick shower with peppermint body wash because that always makes me feel more energized, then I surveyed my meager wardrobe options. I wanted something easy to move in, so nothing too tight. And I wanted something that might help disguise the fact I was wearing my taser.

This was one morning I wasn't about to leave home without it. I'd had too many close calls already. Even if most of them were only in my mind.

I settled on a pair of tan cargo pants and a black tank top covered with an oversized flannel shirt. The plus for the cargo pants was that they had a Velcro-closed compartment that would easily hold my small taser. The fact that the compartment was within fast and easy reach cinched the deal.

Arc woke up as I was tying my sneakers. He rubbed his eyes and yawned. "What time is it?"

"Six o'clock."

His head slumped back down on the pillow. He was lucky. My sofa made a pretty comfortable bed. Otherwise, he'd have had to make do with the cat bed I'd bought for Destiny. It was a nice one too. But, well, he'd have to sleep as a cat. Which wouldn't be a bad thing from where I stood.

"Wake me up when it gets to be a decent hour." He rolled over facing the back of the couch and threw an arm over his eyes, shielding them from the light.

"You'll have to wake your own self up. I'm going out. Probably be gone most of the day too."

He turned his head back to me and opened one eye. "Are you going to a big store?"

"It's not on the agenda at this moment, no. But if I do, I'll remember to pick you up a pair of non flip-flops and some underwear." I paused, grinning. "I guess I should ask—boxers or briefs?"

Another yawn. "Actually, I wear boxer briefs, so in a way, both." Then the eye closed and I swear a second later he was already snoring.

How do people do that? If I get woken up, it takes me forever to go back to sleep. He, apparently, could do it in the blink of an eye. Lucky duck.

I grabbed my keys and my backpack and ran down to the car. As I drove around to the front of the house, Sheriff

Taylor stepped out in front of me. Good thing I was going slow. When I pulled to a stop, he stepped up to the window.

"You got a job you're going to?"

"Just checking some things out." I was still racking my brain to come up with some way to share my information but to no avail. 'My cat told me' just wouldn't work.

He leaned down and rested his forearms on my car door. "What kind of things?"

I took a deep breath. I know that cops and private investigators usually had a bad working relationship, and I was pretty sure that as I wasn't even a licensed investigator yet, there wouldn't even be a working relationship here. Still, it wouldn't hurt for someone to know where I was going. Narrow the field for them if I didn't make it back.

Way to think positive, right?

"I'm going to check out the other coven members that were there the night of the full moon meeting. That has to be when the donut was poisoned, so maybe they saw something that might help."

He gave me a slow smile. "Gee, now why didn't I think of something like that? Questioning possible witnesses to a crime? Wow, what a stellar and never before thought of idea."

I shrugged. "Maybe I can jog their memory. Sometimes people think of things a bit later down the road. It's possible that they've remembered something since they talked with you or one of your men."

The sheriff nodded. "That is possible." Then he glanced over his shoulder. "Why don't you stay here and let me and Trevor do that instead?"

I could tell by the tone of his voice that he knew that was just wishful thinking on his part. I mean, I was dressed, in my car, and headed to the road. I would do this.

"I got this, sheriff, but I promise to be careful. And if I find out anything, you have my word that I'll call you immediately."

That wasn't enough for him. "If you're set on going, then fine." His face took on a determined expression. "But Trevor goes with you." When I opened my mouth, he held up his palm to me. "No arguments. You two either go together, or he follows you everywhere you go. Your choice. But it would save gas if the two of you were in one car."

The apple sure didn't fall far from the tree with Opie and his dad. Each of them was every bit as maddening as the other. Men.

I will hand one thing to the more masculine race, though. They could get ready to go way faster than we could.

Our voices must have carried on the breeze, because by this time Opie was stepping out of the tent, fully dressed in his daily uniform. He held up two fingers toward the car and then darted into the house.

The sheriff looked down at me. "You gonna be sensible about this?"

Did I have a choice? Not the way I saw it. I nodded and put the car in park. Two minutes wouldn't kill me.

When Opie came out, he tried to get me to change vehicles, but I stood firm. I wanted the control of being behind the wheel, and that was something I wouldn't have in Opie's car. No one but him drove his precious baby. Another difference between guys and girls.

When he finally climbed in on the passenger side, I had to do a double take.

"What?" Then he ran a hand over his not normal at all for him five o'clock shadow. "It's the facial hair, isn't it? I'd be happy to shave, but it takes longer than two minutes."

I'd never seen him with stubble before. That elusive part of my heart tweaked again. Goddess help me, but I was starting to fall for my best friend. Heaven help us if it didn't work out well.

"I like it." Then I pulled my eyes off him and handed him my list. "You can be the navigator. These are the addresses of all eight remaining coven members."

Opie glanced at the list as I drove down to the entrance to the road. "You're missing an address, aren't you? He might not be a coven member, but I understand Tommy Hill was there that night too." His voice sounded a little tense when he said it.

"For the start of things, yeah, but he left way before the meeting truly started." Still, Opie was right, he was there and should be included on the list. "I know where he lives. We can save him for last."

"Sure." There was a lot more tension in that one word than I liked. Maybe a little jealousy too?

As I drove into town, I finally caved. It would be so much easier if Opie knew what I was looking for.

"What if I told you I had some information about yesterday, but I couldn't tell you how I got it?"

That got his attention rather quickly. "What kind of information?"

In for a penny, in for a pound my grandmother used to say. "The person who threw those firebombs into the house was wearing a witch's cloak and drove away in a big blue car."

He was struggling, but it was a losing battle from the beginning. "I'm sorry, but how do you know this?" When I hesitated, he got a knowing look on his face. "It's a magic thing, isn't it? Some kind of seeing spell?"

I didn't want to give him the impression we had the ability to see into the past. That would open far too many doors. There might actually be a spell for that somewhere, but it would take a powerful witch to pull it off. More likely at least a trio of powerful witches. A trinity. There wasn't much a trinity couldn't do. As long as they all had magic.

"It wasn't a spell, but I can honestly say that magic is involved in the reason I can't give you a straight answer. Does that help?"

"Not really, but I'm guessing I'll have to make do with that." I nodded. "Okay, so at least tell me this—can we truly rely that this is accurate information?"

I thought about it and then nodded again. Arc really didn't have a reason to lie to me. He wanted this killer caught almost as much as we did, even if his reasoning was more self-centered than ours.

"So, we're looking for a coven member that drives, or has access to, a big blue car." He glanced my way. "Don't suppose you have a make or model?"

"No, just size and color."

"Well, that's something we didn't have before."

Opie gave us a big break by doing the legwork. He called into the sheriff's office and asked them to run the coven members through the Department of Motor Vehicles' database. By the time we hit the main street in town, we had the results. There were only two matches.

Frank Cordoba was one. He was the local jeweler and a mild-mannered man. I had a hard time putting him into the role of a killer. Besides, I just couldn't see any motive for him.

The other was Tammy Tillsdale. She was a little more on the side of suspicious, but not by much. Still, we had to start somewhere. It was still too early to actually go knocking on people's doors, so we opted to grab donuts and coffee at the Flour Pot.

When I saw the full display of Raspberry Delights, I grabbed a half dozen for Opal. Maybe they would help brighten her day a little. Ruby had told me last night that Opal and she would work the full day shift at the shop together and then close up early.

I could totally understand their reasoning. Neither of them wanted the other one very far out of their sight while all of this was going on. I got that. It made me happy in one way that Mom was out gallivanting around the world, and very sad in another. What I wouldn't give for one of her deep bear hugs right now. It was hard going through something like this without someone that had your back.

Opie cleared his throat from across the table, and I looked up to find him smiling at me. "A penny for your thoughts?"

Okay, so maybe someone had my back after all. He was even kind of family. A friendship that's lasted as long as ours has counted as family in my book.

"Sorry. For some reason, this whole thing really has me missing my mom. And I can't even call her to let her know what's going on because I'm not sure where she is. Her cell phone isn't working. All I get is an unavailable message every time I try to call."

"I'm sure she's fine. Your mom is every bit as powerful as Opal in her own way, you know."

"Yeah. I'm just being selfish. I should be happy she's out of harm's way, not wishing her here right into the heart of it."

We munched in silence for a few minutes. Funny, but Opie and I were okay with silence. Maybe because both of us enjoyed our food more than most people did.

As we wound down after our third donut each, Opie's chewing became thoughtful. "You know, there is another possibility we might want to think about. Misty Rhodes drives a big blue Buick, remember?"

I tilted my head at him. "You really think she was capable of doing something this involved when she was in the state she was when we left her?"

"No, but maybe her lover borrowed her car?" He finished the last bite and then continued. "He could have borrowed her cloak too, for that matter. I'm sure he had access to both. Maybe she even left a cloak at his house?"

As much as I wanted to pin this all on Calvin Brenton, it just didn't sound right to me. "I don't know, but it's worth checking out."

I saw his eyes go back to the counter and then to the bag on the table filled with Opal's donuts. I hastily pulled the bag closer to me. "These are for Opal, not you."

He nodded and stood up. "Okay, then let's get out of here before I have to double my gym time tomorrow."

Gym time. What a novel idea. I'd have to check into that sometime.

"Do you mind if we drop these off at the shop first?" It wasn't just Opie's willpower I was worried about. The sooner the donuts were out of our sight, the better.

"Okay by me."

But when we drove up and parked across the street from the front of the shop, the closed sign was still on the front door. That was odd. Opal was adamant about the shop opening at eight sharp and it was now ten minutes past.

My worry went up a notch when Ruby didn't answer her cell phone.

"Do we head back to the farmhouse?" Opie asked.

I took a close look at the shop. Something didn't feel right. "I have a key to the back door. Let's walk around and I'll let us in. If they aren't here, then we'll double back to the farmhouse."

He nodded, and I noticed that his right hand was resting lightly on the butt of his gun as we walked. Yeah, he felt it too.

At the back door, he took the key from me and went to unlock it. That proved unnecessary. The door had been forced open. We looked at each other and my heart fell into my stomach.

Opie pushed the door open, and it gave freely. No bell here, as this was a private entrance. That worked in our favor. He put his finger to his lips, drew his gun and pointed to me and then to the ground at my feet.

Yeah, like that would happen. When he saw my look, he took a deep breath and then pointed behind him. Okay, that I would do.

We heard the voices as soon as we got through the doorway. They were coming from the front of the shop.

"Why are you witches so blasted hard to kill? How many lives do you wretched beasts of Satan have?"

I knew that voice. Naomi Hill.

"Don't worry about your precious little cousin, Amethyst. I'll take care of her just as soon as I'm done here. I'm tired of you horrid creatures befouling our town and bewitching our men. It has to be put to an end."

Opie parted the curtain, and I peeked over his shoulder. Opal was on the ground and Ruby was kneeling beside her, crying. As we watched, she lifted her eyes to a spot to the left that was out of our eyesight. "If you've killed her, I swear to you that you will pay." Then her lips started moving silently.

I knew that Naomi would know what that meant as well as I did. I darted past Opie, pulling my taser as I ran. He cleared the curtain a half second after me.

Our sudden appearance startled Naomi and the end of the shotgun she was holding shifted from Ruby to me. Opie tackled me to the ground just as she pulled the trigger. Buckshot sailed through the air bare inches above us as my taser went rolling across the floor. Before we could get to our feet, Ruby let loose with her spell.

As we watched, the air lit up with a red flash of light and the shotgun started glowing. Naomi cried out in pain and dropped the weapon. Unfortunately, not before she'd pumped it to chamber another round. The damn thing went off again, this time after hitting the ground.

Luckily, the end of the barrel landed mostly pointed toward the back of the shop. Unfortunately, not quite enough so to completely miss both of us.

I could tell from Opie's grunt that he'd been hit, and something inside me boiled. Naomi stared at me in horror as my hair began to float.

At least this time I had a clear target.

Chapter 24

"Amie, no!"

I heard the cry from behind me, but it was too late. My hands were raised, and the magic was already slamming out of me. Not that I would I have stopped it if even if I could have. Naomi Hill deserved this.

Sparkling air picked her up and threw her against the wall, directly on top of a hanging display of antique quilts. She hung there, her eyes bulging and her hands clawing at her throat.

My eyes were still focused on her, and my hands still up and out in front of me.

"Let her go, Amie." Opal's soft voice came from behind me still. I risked a quick glance to make sure she was really okay and found her propped up on her elbow, still on the floor. Her eyes were wide, but her voice was calm. "You're better than she is, Amie. Let her go."

The magic didn't want to let go. Truthfully, I didn't want to let go. I wanted nothing more than to kill the

189

woman who had tried to eradicate my entire family. She deserved to die. And she deserved to die by magic.

Ruby's hand touched my shoulder. "Just breathe and lower your hands."

It was so much harder to do than I could ever have imagined, but I did. Once my hands were down at my side, Naomi dropped like a stone. Gasping for breath, she started trying to crawl away from me.

I lifted one finger and wagged it at her and she froze. "That's better."

"Ruby, I think I dropped my taser. Would you please get it for me?" I put as much sweetness as I could into my request, but she knew me too well. She picked it up, but she held on to it. That worked just as well for me. Well, almost anyway.

I turned and looked down at Opie. I'd thought Opal's eyes were wide, but they were nothing compared to his. Yeah, you think you know a person.

"Are you okay?" I asked softly, hating the sheer fear I saw in his eyes.

He nodded, then winced. After a couple of deep breaths, he pointed to his leg. "I took a little buckshot, but I don't think anything is broken."

"Good. Call your dad. I want that woman out of my sight." My eyes went to the sniveling creature still huddled against the wall shaking. I smiled at her. "I don't suggest you try to jump bail, either, should it even be offered to you. I will find you."

She swallowed and nodded.

I walked toward the back room. I could feel the weakness coming over me. The curtain barely closed behind me before I went down.

***

When I came to this time, all I noticed for the first few minutes was the pain. Growing a tree was nothing compared to this. I had to learn how to control this magic. And I had to learn fast. Preferably before I did something stupid in the heat of the moment that I couldn't undo.

Like kill someone. Whether they deserved it or not wasn't the issue. With the magic not filling my head and body, I could see that.

"I know you're with us again, Amie." That was Opal's voice. "The sheriff here needs to talk with you for a minute before he takes Opie over to the hospital emergency room. We don't want to keep him waiting, now do we?"

I shook my head. Big mistake. The pain flared, and I almost screamed. She shoved a couple of pills into my hand quickly followed by a glass of water. "Take these, they will help."

Then she placed my head between her palms and chanted briefly under her breath. The pain didn't exactly go away, but it retreated just far enough that I could think again.

Sheriff Taylor stepped up beside Opal. "I've already gotten brief statements from the others, and Naomi Hill is on her way to a nice iron cell in my jail. Where, if I have anything to say about, she'll be spending a heck of a lot of time before we transfer her to a more serious place." He paused, and the look he gave me wasn't unkindly. Of course, he hadn't seen what happened either.

"Can you tell me what happened from your viewpoint?"

I nodded and told him the story minus the magical part. It wasn't lying to say I shoved her into the wall. That's exactly what I did. The fact that magic was involved surely couldn't be all that relevant in the end, could it?

When I finished, he nodded. "Pretty much what the others said happened. Good to see you all have your stories straight." He flashed me a quick smile. "Would you believe Naomi is insisting you threw her from across the room?" He shook his head. "Her hatred must have finally driven her around the bend. Don't know if she'll make it back this time."

Truthfully? I didn't care. She was alive and so were we. That was all that mattered to me right now.

Well, almost.

"Can I see Opie for a minute before you guys leave? Alone?"

"I have an even better idea than that." Opie was standing in the doorway, leaning heavily on a wooden cane. Someone had wrapped his leg to help control the bleeding, but the wrap was already turning red. "Dad really needs to get back to the office to deal with this. Think maybe you're up to driving me?"

Opal didn't look so sure about that, but I nodded quickly. I think maybe I even managed to hide the wince from the pain it brought.

"Absolutely."

When Opal opened her mouth to protest, Ruby stepped in. "I'll drive and the two of you can ride in the back." She glanced at her mom. "Would that be okay?"

Opal gave me a close once over, then nodded. "Keep an eye on her, you hear?"

"I will."

I gave Ruby the keys and climbed in the back seat with Opie. We were halfway to the next town, and the hospital, before either of us said a word.

Not that I didn't want to. It was that I had no idea how to start the conversation.

"So you really weren't kidding when you said you could do magic now, huh?"

My head was turned toward the window, watching the scenery flash past. I couldn't bear to see his expression right now. Would things ever be the same between us?

I shrugged. "I think I just lucked out and got a super magical cat or something. I'm not all that sure the magic is mine." Which brought up a good point. Someone needed to check on Arc and make sure he was okay.

Ruby's eyes met mine in the rearview mirror. Like I said, my cousin had always been able to read me.

"Your cat is fine, trust me." It was the way she said it. I knew she'd talked to him. That made me feel better.

"How's your leg?" I said, putting my attention to where it should have been all along.

"Painful. Your aunt gave me some pills though when she was wrapping it up and it's at least bearable now."

Yeah, it was the pills that did that. But letting him think that wasn't going to hurt anything.

After that, we went back to silence. Not the comfortable kind of silence we normally had between us either. Something had changed. Shifted. Maybe Opie had never really believed us all these years about magic really existing. Or maybe he just couldn't cope with the fact that I wasn't the person he had thought I was.

How could I tell him all this was new to me too?

When we pulled up to the emergency entrance, Opie climbed out and then waved us off. His eyes had a closed off look to them. "You two get back to Opal. I'll take it from here." Then he turned and walked away. I waited outside the glass doors until I saw him reach the front desk, then I got into the front seat beside Ruby.

My vision was blurring.

It took a while for me to realize that's because I was crying.

Chapter 25

I forced myself to neatly fold my jeans before I stuffed them into my suitcase. They'd end up wrinkled anyway, but at least I could say I tried. Hopefully, there would be access to a washer and dryer at the other end of the journey.

It had been two days now since the magic show at Opal's shop. Naomi Hill was in jail for the foreseeable future, as Boswell Bonds had refused to help her out with bail money. I'd like to think he did that for me, but I think he just knew she was one heck of a flight risk.

The thing that bothered me most was that I hadn't seen or talked to Opie since we dropped him off at the hospital. This was officially the longest time we'd been apart since the day I met him. And it hurt like crazy. At least his dad had let us know that he was okay. The buckshot had missed the important parts. Thank the Goddess for that.

Opal and Ruby both tell me that he'll come around in time, but I'm not at all sure of that. I know what he saw back there, and it wasn't a sane and law-abiding witch. It was a crazy maniac that would have gleefully killed her victim and spit out the bones. Well, you know what I mean. It wasn't the girl he thought he knew, that's the main thing.

Trouble was, it wasn't the me I knew either. Magic was changing me, and I wasn't at all sure it was a change for the better.

This trip couldn't have come at a better time. Of course, if it wasn't for Arc, I wouldn't have this blasted magic, and therefore I wouldn't need to leave.

To say I was conflicted would be vastly understating my feelings.

"Are you sure you're up to this?" Ruby pulled at the chenille on my bedspread. "I might be able to talk Opal into giving me a week off from the shop." She pulled a face. "She makes all the decisions there, anyway."

I shook my head. As much as I appreciated her offer, I didn't want my family around me until I got this thing under control. The last thing in the world I wanted was to hurt them somehow.

"I'll be okay. And I'll have Arc."

"She really did deserve it, you know."

I knew that, but it still didn't mean I should have reacted the way I did.

Once we knew it was Naomi, all the clues had started dancing around us, mocking us for not having noticed them before. The fact that Misty saw her big blue car pass her on the way back to town that night. The fact that her husband George had access to syringes as he was diabetic. The borrowed witch's cloak hanging in Tommy's closet. Shoot, she was even there when I bought the blasted donut that started all this.

And the thing that had finally sent her on the final leg of crazy? Her son Tommy admitting that he liked me and telling her he wanted her to lay off the witch hunt.

Yeah. Didn't work out quite the way he'd wanted it to.

"You almost ready?" Arc's voice was soft and questioning. He'd been walking and talking very softly around me ever since that fateful day that changed everything. Like he was afraid that if he startled me, I'd blast him or something. And who knows? Maybe the new magical me would do something like that.

I was really starting to not like her very much.

"Yeah. You sure your uncle will be okay with this?"

He shrugged. "I can't very well call him, not even from your phone. I know within reason they have his lines tapped. They'll be monitoring his calls."

I knew he wasn't talking about the local law enforcement. He was talking about the council. Funny, a week ago, the thought of coming up against the witches' council would have had me shaking in my boots.

Not today. Today, I just wanted answers to a lot of things. Maybe I'd get some, maybe I wouldn't. But Arc had promised me that he would help me learn to control the magic along the way. I was counting on that.

Plus, we really needed to find a way to break the binding between us. If we could do that, I could go back to being magic-less Amie.

I missed her.

Oh yeah, and we had to figure out what had really happened to Sonya and clear Arc's name. I knew that was his main priority. It should have been mine too, but it wasn't. Not really.

I wanted the magic gone.

The End... For Now

Want the next book? <u>Relatively Familiar is now available for Pre-Order.</u> (Click link to go to Amazon's product page.) Will go live on August 30th!

A Note From Belinda

Thank you so much for reading All Too Familiar. I truly hope you enjoyed it! Please check out my website at BelindaWrites.com for updates on upcoming books.

Also, if you can spare a few minutes, please consider giving my book a review. I'd really appreciate knowing what you thought of it.

Belinda White
August 2019

Made in the USA
San Bernardino, CA
26 January 2020